SPECIAL MESSAGE TO READERS

THE ULVERSCROFT FOUNDATION
(registered UK charity number 264873)

was established in 1972 to provide funds for research, diagnosis and treatment of eye diseases. Examples of major projects funded by the Ulverscroft Foundation are:-

- The Children's Eye Unit at Moorfields Eye Hospital, London
- The Ulverscroft Children's Eye Unit at Great Ormond Street Hospital for Sick Children
- Funding research into eye diseases and treatment at the Department of Ophthalmology, University of Leicester
- The Ulverscroft Vision Research Group, Institute of Child Health
- Twin operating theatres at the Western Ophthalmic Hospital, London
- The Chair of Ophthalmology at the Royal Australian College of Ophthalmologists

You can help further the work of the Foundation by making a donation or leaving a legacy. Every contribution is gratefully received. If you would like to help support the Foundation or require further information, please contact:

THE ULVERSCROFT FOUNDATION
**The Green, Bradgate Road, Anstey
Leicester LE7 7FU, England
Tel: (0116) 236 4325**

website: www.foundation.ulverscroft.com

THE VIGILANCE
COMMITTEE WAR

A gang of vigilantes calling themselves the Vigilance Committee are preventing part of the Indian Territory from becoming a state, and former Texas Rangers Buck Armstrong and Louie Lewis are being paid by local businesses to bring them in. Making their job difficult is the fact that most of the area's ranchers don't care, or approve of the hangings carried out by the Committee. When the pards get too close to Committee members, Louie himself ends up at the end of a hangman's noose . . .

BILL SHEEHY

♦

THE VIGILANCE COMMITTEE WAR

Complete and Unabridged

LINFORD
Leicester

First published in Great Britain in 2017 by
Robert Hale
an imprint of The Crowood Press
Wiltshire

First Linford Edition
published 2019
by arrangement with
The Crowood Press
Wiltshire

A catalogue record for this book is available
from the British Library.

ISBN 978–1–4448–4239–5

Published by
F. A. Thorpe (Publishing)
Anstey, Leicestershire

Set by Words & Graphics Ltd.
Anstey, Leicestershire
Printed and bound in Great Britain by
T. J. International Ltd., Padstow, Cornwall

This book is printed on acid-free paper

1

The tree growing close to the edge of the trail was different than any of the others in that little grove. An old oak, its trunk was huge and the branches, those low down, were as big around as a man's thigh. The thing that set this tree out was the sign nailed to the rough bark of the trunk.

The two men riding down the well-worn dirt roadway had been lazing along, taking their time, discussing things of no consequence. Seeing the white paper sign and the rope tied off from one of the massive limbs changed all that.

'What the hell . . . ?' exclaimed one of the pair. 'Now ain't that something?'

Both men sat their saddles, looking first at the dangling rope and then reading the sign.

'Well, Buck, guess we're getting close

1

to where we're going. Wouldn't ya say?'

'Uh huh. Looks like it.'

The two were as different as day and night. James Buckley Armstrong, known simply as Buck to his friends, was a big man. Even sitting in a saddle it was obvious he was a cattleman. Standing slightly over six-feet tall in his stocking feet, when he could afford socks, his erect posture in the saddle made it obvious he had some military experience in his background. It was equally clear he spent as little time as possible on his feet. He was most comfortable on a horse. Now, in his trail-worn denim pants, faded red shirt and scarred boots with rundown heels it was clear he was a cattleman.

His partner was shorter, heavier and part Mexican. Answering to Louie, this man had his father to thank for his name. A German emigrant, the elder Lewis arrived in central Texas shortly before the Republic became the 28th state. A teacher of languages looking for adventure, he was hired by a wealthy Mexican ranching family to teach their children. In short order he fell in love with the lovely Gabriela Garza. The first born of this match was christened Aloysius Lewis. Today few people knew him by that name. His pa, reportedly laughing at the time, named him Aloysius knowing it was the Latinisation of the name Louie. Louie Lewis. Pa had had a great sense of humour.

There was little humour in the sign or the rope. A hangman's noose had been tied in the rope. The sign made the message clear: 'Warning! Anyone caught rustling livestock, the Vigilance Committee will hang you with your own rope'.

'Now ain't that something?' said Louie, settling back and rolling a quirley. 'Ya think it's aimed at us?'

Buck took the makings from a shirt pocket and rolled his own smoke. 'I doubt it,' he said after touching a match to the end. 'It isn't likely anyone on this so-called Committee would know we'd been hired. Or even we were on our way.'

'I still wonder about that. Us being hired to stop this bunch of vigilantes from doing what they been doing. Doesn't Auburn have a sheriff?'

'Yeah, it does. But the sheriff is limited to taking care of law things within the town limits. According to Winterbottom there's some kind of territorial marshal but that person stays pretty close to the governor's office down in the territorial capital. Looks as if it's left up to the folks living beyond the town limits to take care of things themselves.'

'So? Ain't that what this Vigilance Committee is doing? I guess I'm not too sure exactly what vigilantes are all about.'

'Well, back in Texas, riding for the Rangers, we didn't have much truck with such things. However, get out in some of the communities far from town, or some of the ranches out in the flats, there aren't a lot of lawmen to keep things under control. Now the letter I got hiring us said this so-called Vigilance Committee has gotten too powerful. Deciding on their own who to hang whether they are caught rustling or not. Likely we'll know more after we talk to this Winterbottom fellow.'

'Well it sure looks as if we could find ourselves caught in the middle of something if we ain't careful.'

Buck smiled and reined his horse back onto the road. 'Uh huh. We'll just have to make sure we keep our eyes open.'

2

The two took their time, enjoying the light breeze that had sprung up bringing the smell of wild flowers and untrampled grasslands. Since leaving northern Texas they had ridden through an ever changing landscape. From the dryness of the Texas plains up into the higher prairie of the Indian Territory where they found better grazing country and even, in the higher mountain ranges, thick forests.

The road they took coming out of the territorial capital, Fort Rawlins, was well defined, being used by farm wagons, stage coaches and herds of cattle being driven to market. At one place, not far from the town they were riding to, Auburn, the road ran alongside a river. Not a big river, such as those they were more familiar with like the Rio Grande or the Brazos, but still too big to be considered merely a creek.

'Bet there's some good fishing there,' said Louie, stopping in the middle of a wide log bridge to look down into the water.

'Now tell the truth, Louie, when's the last time you went fishing? Fact is, have you ever gone fishing?'

Louie laughed. 'Nope, can't say I have. Doesn't make much sense to me, putting a worm on a hook and then sitting patiently for a hungry fish to come by. Anyway, I'm not sure I'd want to eat something that fed on worms. Would you?'

'No, but then I've had some darn good meals with fish and oysters and the like and I never questioned what kinds of things they ate. Think of the bacon you like at breakfast time. Ever think about what mud that hog the bacon came from had wallowed in? Best not to think about things like that.'

The two men laughed and rode on,

enjoying each other's company and the day.

Riding on into Auburn the two stopped at the far edge of town to look the place over. Not a big town, from what they could see all the businesses fronted on both sides of one wide street. Thick dust from the dirt street made the false-fronted buildings all look to have been painted with the same brush.

'Town could use a good rain storm,' said Louie, 'wash some of that dust off everything.'

'From the looks of things, it's been a while since there's been any rain. But look there, all the way in today, all the grasslands have been high and green. Must be a lotta ground water.'

'Well, we're here. So what do we do now?'

'I'd say we take care of ourselves then go have a talk with Winterbottom. He's the mayor so I reckon he's got a good handle on things.'

Riding down the main street they read the painted signs, noting where the sheriff's office was, and the bank and the hotel. At the far end of the businesses was a huge barn.

'I reckon these horses could use a good feed and maybe a brushing. I spotted a Chinese laundry back there. Probably got public baths out back.'

'Then it's to that restaurant. Gawd, I'm so tired of your cooking, I could spit.'

Buck laughed. 'You weren't complaining this morning. I noticed you didn't leave much behind on your tin plate.'

Climbing stiffly out of the saddle, Buck nodded to the old timer standing in the livery's double doorway. 'Afternoon. We'd like to feed and brush out our animals.'

'Wal, I reckon. Cost ya two-bits a piece. Cash money up front.'

Smiling, Buck dug into a pocket and brought out some coins. The livery man took them and nodded. 'Wal, for an extry two-bits I'll do the brushing fer ya.'

'Thanks but no,' said the big man. 'Fact is I'd better warn you. This horse of mine don't like people much. He's got a bad temper and, well, I'd stay a long way off from him, was I you.'

'Ah, teach your mother to suck eggs, young fella. I been around horses man and boy. Ain't see one yet what I can't handle.'

Louie laughed and started stripping the saddle from his big brown gelding. 'Buck, if'n I was you I'd go ahead and let this old coot try his hand. That black stud horse of yours would teach him a lesson.'

'Naw, I can't do that, Louie.' Turning to the old man, Buck nodded. 'You got to be careful of Ol' Horse here, front and back. Has a bad habit of biting and kicking, he does.' Picking up a stiff-bristled brush from a shelf he started brushing the black's dusty hide, always keeping one eye on the animal's nose.

The horse wasn't a great beauty, but

he and Buck had been partners for a long time and both knew about the other. Thinking about it as he worked, Buck chuckled. Horse was hard mouthed, strong willed and pigheaded, that was for sure. He'd warned the old wrangler of the animal's bad temper but hadn't mentioned how thin his tolerance was for the man who rode him. Buck knew given the chance Ol' Horse would take a hunk out of his butt.

Leaving the horses with a bait of oats and the freedom of the corrals out back, the two men headed down the street toward the restaurant.

Starting with mugs of steaming hot coffee, they were just putting knife and fork to thick slabs of half-cooked beef steaks when the restaurant door opened and a man pushed though. Louie glanced at the man, then looked to make sure Buck saw him. He had.

Barely able to pass through the doorway without turning sideways, the man waddled into the room. Waddled,

Louie thought, walking like a duck, swaying side to side with each step. Short and round, the man's body was curved from shoulder to ankle. Wearing a pinstriped suit, the buttons on his vest looked to be about to bust free. His head, bald and as round as his body, was perched on almost non-existent shoulders like a billiard ball balanced on a melon.

'Gentlemen,' the newcomer said, pulling a chair around and sitting at the table. 'Let me introduce myself. I'm William J. Winterbottom, mayor of this fine community. I would guess you are James B. Armstrong and Louie Lewis. Is that not correct?'

Louie almost choked, having just taken a mouthful of beef. Buck swallowed and nodded.

'Yes,' said the big man slowly, 'you guessed right. My partner, Louie, and I'm Buck Armstrong.' He hesitated a moment before putting a hand out to shake.

'Ah, good. I've been watching for

you. Have to get something done, you know. Can't be having people stringing up people right, left and centre. Not good for business, you understand. No sir. Not good at all.'

Not to be bothered by the interruption, the two men went back to cutting pieces off their steaks and continued eating.

'Yes,' said the mayor after a moment, 'I shouldn't be bothering you while you're having your meal. I apologize. However, it is important you succeed with your job as soon as possible. There are a lot of things at stake here. Yes, indeed. Big things. Big for Auburn and for the state.'

Buck finished chewing and stopped. 'State? I thought this was still a territory? When did it become a state?'

'Well . . . ' The rotund man fidgeted, one hand dry-washing the other as he stammered, 'Yes. You are right. We are a territory. But that will change. Yes sir,' he said gathering up steam, 'statehood can't be far away. All the important people, the business people, you know, throughout the territory are working hard to that end. Statehood, gentlemen, means a lot for this part of this great country of ours.'

'Uh, *señor*,' said Louis sounding more Mexican than ever, 'is what you want us to do part of that? Getting the territory to become a state?'

'Yes, sir. A mighty big part. However it is doubtful the US Congress will approve of statehood if reports of men getting hung continue to be heard. It is vital your work is done and done as quickly as possible.'

Turning to Buck, Louie grimaced. 'You see, *mi compadre*? I told you to ask for more money for this little job. Didn't I? *Sí*. I did. Now we have lost that opportunity. Now we do this job and ride away with only a few dollars in our pockets when we could have been rich. *Sí*. Rich.'

'Well,' said Winterbottom, holding his hands up, 'we have an agreement. We settled on the terms. Don't think you can come in here and hold us up. No sir. Our business people who are fronting this effort won't see to it. No sir.'

Louie, slowly shaking his head, looked sad. '*Sí, señor. Yo comprende.* We have agreed. We will do the job for the amount agreed on.' Quickly holding out his hand, he smiled evilly at the mayor. 'Now is a good time for us to be paid, no?'

'Uh, uh, well, yes. I suppose. However I don't have the money on me. Not right this minute.'

Buck cut in. 'That's all right. We'll wait a bit for our money. Meanwhile, once we finish up with our lunch, we'd like to sit down and talk about things.'

'It is simple; we want you to get rid of the so-called Vigilance Committee. They are destroying our town. Our businesses. Calling people rustlers and hanging them. It has to cease.'

'And the good people here don't know who they are? Don't they care about what this committee of vigilantes is doing?'

Back to dry-washing his hands, it was the mayor's turn to look sad. 'These are good people, yes indeed. But still . . . I hate to say it, but still there are some who think the Vigilance Committee is doing the right thing. Yes, it's hard to believe, but, well, I've heard some talk from some pretty important people who think vigilance committees to be 'popular tribunals' and are necessary to protect life and property. Why, just recently,' said the man getting a little excited in his talk, 'in an article in the *Auburn Journal*, the editor lamented the rustling of livestock. He went so far as to write something — here, let me read it to you.' Taking a piece of paper from a pocket, he adjusted his glasses and started reading. ''It is high time a quietus in the shape of a good hemp rope and a high tree limb is administered to stop such proceedings'.' Putting the paper back in his pocket, he frowned. 'It is hard to admit, but it is the truth, not everyone sees the Vigilance Committee as being a bad thing. And believe it or not, some of those are among the business people who are paying you. Yes, some of them hope you fail and will likely do what they can to stop you from succeeding.'

3

Louie glanced first at his partner before staring hard at the man. 'We are going to get paid, aren't we?'

'Oh, most definitely. Yes. Let me assure you of that. What I mean is, well, take for instance Handley Runkle. He has the Double Bar R ranch. One of the two large spreads that supports this community. Oh, there are a handful of other, smaller cattle and horse outfits, but the Double Bar R and the Frying Pan are the big boys. Now, Mr Runkle doesn't believe he's losing much beef to rustlers. Says his hired hands can take care of things. However, he wants to support the community so has agreed to pay his share of the pot raised for you.'

Buck, pushing his empty plate away, nodded and sipped his coffee. 'Let me understand this. Nobody knows who

18

this committee of vigilantes are. You hired us to find out and put a stop to their hangings. Just how many rustlers have been hanged by this gang?'

'Well,' said the mayor, looking for the first time uncomfortable, 'nobody's sure. I mean until, oh, say six months or so back, there would be rumours of some fella getting hung from a tree after being caught with cattle that didn't belong to him. It's only kinda recently there's been a half-dozen or so men found hanging at various places but, well, some aren't sure a couple of them were really rustlers. That's the problem. Doesn't seem to matter to this Committee. Pinned to each of the dead men's shirts they left a note, warning would-be rustlers that they'd be next.'

'What do you mean?'

'Well, not all the hangings were anywhere near any cattle. Or even out on someone's range. More'n one was found out on open range. There's a lot of open range, you know. Simply grasslands nobody's bothered to put markers on. That makes it hard to know who owns any cattle out there. I'm a storekeeper and don't know much about livestock, but I'm told cattle like to spread out, eating here and there as they go.'

Buck nodded. 'Yeah, they don't pay much attention, just like to move around a bit. So these big spreads you mentioned, Frying Pan and Double Bar R, they rely on open range?'

'Oh, yes. Yes, indeed. Why the Frying Pan, just a bit east of here, Martin Jacobson owns that, he's only got the 160 acres he was allowed to file on. But backing up against the foothills like he does, he has a corner on another huge amount of federal land.'

'I imagine this causes problems for the Committee - I mean catching someone putting a brand on a maverick might be misunderstood.'

'Exactly. Yes, that is what I think has happened. If someone was caught rounding up a bunch of unbranded cattle out on the open range, say in the spring before there was a roundup, well, would that be rustling? Who's to say they weren't simply gathering wild stock? But that's not likely for either of the big spreads. Both Runkle and Jacobson got here before anyone. They put down their claim markers for 160 acres as allowed under the Homestead Act. Old Runkle, he's a sly old dog, he had his hired hands make claims adjacent and then bought those claims. To make it all work both ranches are able to control huge acreages of open range that way. Out there, miles from anywhere is where rustlers do their work. At least that's what that damn Committee claims.'

'Well,' said Buck, standing up and putting a few coins on the table, 'I don't imagine we'll get much done simply riding out hoping to catch anyone stringing some poor fool to a tree limb. We'll have to find another way to get what you want. OK, Mr Winterbottom, we'll start earning our money.'

Shaking hands with the shorter man,

Buck and Louie pushed out, stopping on the sidewalk to settle their hats.

'And what,' asked Louie, adjusting his Stetson to the right angle, 'are you thinking of doing to start this search for vigilantes?'

'First off I want a bath. Then some clean clothes. But first I think a drink might be in order. To settle our meal, you understand.'

'Bravo. My thought exactly.'

'Oh, and that Mex talk you were laying on back there, wasn't that a bit heavy?'

'Naw. Mr Mayor wanted to come on as Mr Important. I just wanted to make him think I was impressed. You know, the dumb, lazy Mexicano in awe of the big man?'

Buck chuckled. Then stopped, looking at a group of riders tying up at the saloon hitchrail across the street. 'Hey, Louie, look who just rode in.'

His partner casually glanced across the wide dirt road and let his hand fall to the grips of his hand gun. 'Is that who I think it is? What the hell is he doing here?'

'Yeah, for sure it's Isaac Black. Seeing him after hearing about a gang of rustlers makes me wonder if maybe our job won't be a little easier than we thought. C'mon. Let's go have that drink.'

Louie pulled his Colt and spun the cylinder, checking the loads. 'We go over there, it might be a good idea to have your six-gun handy.'

4

The men had served as Texas Rangers for a handful of years and had developed a standard method for entering a possible dangerous situation. Before stepping across the wide wood sidewalk and going into the saloon, Buck waited for a long minute or two.

Using his left hand he pushed through the swinging doors and quickly stepped to one side, out of the open doorway. Glancing quickly around, he took in the room. A long plank bar was backed up by shelves of bottles and a big mirror. Tables of various sizes, each with spindle-backed chairs, were scattered around the rest of the room. Sunlight from the front windows lit up the front part of the room, the back half was dark in shadow. The place was empty except for the bartender, his dirty white apron ballooning out over a round stomach, and six men seated at a table near the back.

Nodding at the bartender then quickly at the seated men, Buck thumbed the thong off the dogeared hammer of the Colt Dragoon holstered low on his right hip.

'Will you look at what the cat drug in,' said Isaac Black loudly, coming out of his chair to stand facing Buck. 'Men, we are in the company of one of the famous Texas Rangers' celebrated outlaw-catchers. Oh, wait a minute. No, as I recall, the man standing there was once celebrated, but then, lordy me, can you believe? The Rangers fired him!'

Black carefully kept his hand far from his cross-draw holster. Standing relaxed he was almost laughing. 'Yeah, the story I got was he was given a direct order by his boss Ranger and told the fella to go to hell. Is that right, Buck?'

Slowly shaking his head, Buck never took his eyes off the other man.

'Well, I swear,' Black went on,

laughter still backing up his words, 'the famous Buck Armstrong, here in little old Auburn town. Say, Buck, I'm told you're here to end the hanging of rustlers. Is that true?' Waving a hand at another man now standing at his side, he went on, 'Let me introduce you to Son Runkle. Yes, sir, it's his pa who's helping pay for your services. Son, meet Buck Armstrong.'

Buck didn't take his eyes off Black.

The man identified as Son Runkle wasn't smiling. 'I don't care if Pa is paying or not, we don't need no fancy Ranger coming in to fight our battles.' Hitching his gunbelt to a comfortable setting, he snarled, 'Fact is, I ain't so feared of any Ranger.'

Black chuckled. 'Son, there's a couple things I gotta say before you go getting yourself killed. First off, like I told of Buck here, last time we was talking, I'm the one gonna punch his ticket. He caused me no end of grief. And second, if'n you're gonna talk like that, move away. I don't want any bullets coming my way cause of your loose mouth. And finally, think on it. Every time, where you see Buck here, somewhere nearby is his partner, Louie.' He called out, 'Hey, Louie, you still backing up this upstanding man?'

From the back of the room, standing at the end of the bar, Louie laughed. 'Yep, and I still got both Colts primed and ready.'

Son Runkle spun around but stopped when he saw the wide-shouldered man standing calmly, holding a six-gun in each hand.

Black glanced back, then laughed and patted the other man on the back.

'Best you just relax, Son. Ain't gonna be no shooting in here today. Boys,' he looked over his shoulder at the other men, 'I'd say we should be drinking up and getting back to the ranch. We'll save all this for another time.' Looking back at Buck he nodded, 'And for sure Buck Armstrong, there'll be another time for you and me.'

Buck stepped to one side as the

cowboys filed past, pushing through the doors. He watched through the window as they gathered up the reins and climbed aboard their horses. Not moving until the riders, still in a bunch, cantered down the street and out of town.

'Thought there for a minute,' said Louie after coming down to where Buck was standing at the bar, 'we were going to have a war. As I recall that Isaac Black swore he'd shoot you next time y'all met up. Think he got over that?'

Buck nodded at the bartender. 'Bring us a couple glasses of your better beer, will you?' Turning to his partner he smiled, 'Nope, I somehow don't think so. Sooner or later he'll come calling, but I know him. It won't be until he thinks he's got the advantage.'

The bartender sat the glasses in front of the two men and picked up the coins Buck dropped on the bar.

'Tell me,' asked Buck after thanking the man and taking a sip of beer, 'is that one, Son Runkle, really the son of the rancher who owns the Double Bar R?'

'Uh huh,' the bartender mumbled and picking up a greasy rag, started wiping a place on the bar. 'And it ain't often he'll back down from a fight. He likes to push people around, he does. Got a bad attitude.'

Louie wiped foam from his upper lip. 'Is that really his name? Son?'

The bartender chuckled. 'It is. The way I heard it, when it came time to name his newly born son, his pa, Handley Runkle, he wanted to call the boy the same as himself. But he didn't like the idea of there being a junior in the family so he named him Son Handley Runkle. Him being Pa Handley Runkle. Don't make much sense to me, but there it is.'

The explanation got a quiet laugh out of both men. Sipping his beer, Buck smiled at the bartender. 'Well, while we're having a neighbourly conversation, what can you tell us about this committee of vigilantes?'

'Not much. It all started up about a year or so back. Someone found a man hanging from a tree limb not far outa town. A piece of paper pinned to the dead'uns shirt said something about there being one less rustler. Since then there's been a slew of them. Not all with the paper, but most were. And not only at what folks are calling the hanging tree, neither. A couple were spotted on down by the creek bottom and one or two farther out.'

Buck nodded. 'Coming in we saw a sign nailed to a big gnarly oak tree warning rustlers to keep riding. I reckon that's the only warning this gang gives.'

'Uh huh. Been one man strung up there. One of the early ones. Somehow it don't seem right, hanging a man so far from any cattle and claiming he was a rustler. But don't get me wrong. I don't know nothing. I just pour liquor and mind my own business.'

Back out in the sunshine, the two men decided to walk across to the

Chinaman's to bathe. Getting the road dust washed from their clothes while in the tub was part of the clean-up process.

Crossing the dirt street, kicking up dust with each step, neither were paying any attention and were nearly knocked down when a horse-drawn buggy came barrelling around a corner, almost tipping over.

'Hey,' yelled Buck, pushing Louie out of the way. Grabbing at the horse's harness he planted both heels in the dirt. 'Whoa there, whoa up.'

Once the rig was halted, he moved forward to hold the animal's cheek strap.

'Get your hands off my horse,' yelled the driver, grabbing the whip stock and popping it over the horse's back. 'Get out of my way.'

Buck turned the horse's head, gently talking to the animal, calming it down.

Louie, after picking himself up, started to dust himself off but stopped when the whip cracked a second time.

Jumping up onto the buggy step he reached out and jerked the whip from the driver.

'What the hell are you doing?' he snarled. Then looking up into the eyes of a beautiful young woman, he stopped, stunned.

'You fools,' the woman, now standing and jerking the reins one way and then the other, hollered, 'get out of my way. Let loose of my horse. Damn you, can't you see I'm in a hurry?'

Buck gently scratched at the horse's nose, ignored her and continued talking calmly.

'Yes m'am,' said Louie, trying not to stare. He'd seen beautiful women before but nothing like this one. Young, he put her age at maybe sixteen. Long, unbound blonde hair hung inches over her shoulders, when not whipping around as she shook with rage. Dust didn't completely cover her checkered long-sleeved blouse, the tails tucked into the waist of a long flowing woollen skirt. Louie, sure he was in love, handed the whip to the angry young woman as if presenting her with a present.

'All right now,' said Buck, walking back, patting the heavily breathing horse's rump. 'What fire are you rushing to that nearly killing your horse is warranted?'

'It's none of your business. If you're so drunk you can't cross the street you shouldn't be allowed off the sidewalk. Now get out of my way.'

'Wonderful. Louie, have you ever seen anything like it? Such anger. And from such a pretty face, too. Why I do believe someone ought to turn this youngster over a knee and teach her a lesson.'

'Why you . . . ' she started to say, then stopped. 'Do you know who I am? Nobody talks to me that way. And certainly nobody turns me over any knee and lives to brag about it.'

'No m'am,' said Louie, smiling his most pleasant smile. 'It would be a pleasure to be the one who tames such a fiery temper but to do so with love, not force.'

'Bah, no ragtag cowhand will ever lay a hand on me. Now get out of my way. I have important business to conduct.'

'Ragtag cowhand?' said Buck, looking down at his trail-worn clothes. 'Yes, m'am, I reckon we fit that description. But looks are deceiving. For instance look at yourself. From all appearances one would think you are a gentle, well-mannered young lady. But I don't know. Louie, what do you think, a spoiled brat? Seems most likely, wouldn't you say?'

'I'll have you know I'm Rose Marie Jacobson. My father owns the biggest cattle and horse ranch in this part of the territory. When he hears how two saddle tramps accosted his daughter he'll be hanging you out to dry. Now let go of my horse.'

Grabbing the whip she snapped the tippet over the horse's back. The startled animal bolted, sending the buggy down the dusty street in a near panic.

'Oh, boy,' said Buck, watching the buggy disappear in the dust cloud, 'how about that? First we meet the son of one of the men paying us to do a job and now the daughter of another. Not a good way to start, wouldn't you say?'

5

Clean from sitting in a tub of water out behind the Chinaman's, and wearing clothes washed dirt-free from the same place, Buck felt like a new man. Finishing the job by sitting in a barber's chair with a warm towel covering his chin, Buck thought about how to start doing what they'd been hired to do.

'You know, Louie? I reckon having a talk with the local lawman would be about right,' he said, the words, coming from under a warm towel, muffled.

'Sheriff McDonald?' asked the barber, whipping his cut-throat razor against the leather strop. 'I dunno what good that'll do. Now I ain't saying Mac ain't a good enough sheriff, cause he is. But,' he went on talking as he removed the steaming towel and bushed Buck's lower face with white shaving cream, 'for a town this size, wal, there just ain't much sheriffing needed. No sir, and that's a fact.'

Buck, thinking about the sharp straight-edged razor caressing his face, didn't respond. Sitting nearby and watching, Louie did, wanting to keep the man gossiping.

'But if the town don't need a lawman,' he asked, 'why is there even a sheriff?'

'Oh, a couple good reasons. Yes, sir. First off, what kind of town would this be if it didn't have a sheriff? It'd be like if we didn't have a bank . . . or . . . or a saloon. No, sir. Without certain services it wouldn't be no kind of town at all. Then there is a call for the sheriff to do his duty. Not often, mind you, but, wal, there are times. That's when it calls for someone like ol' Mac to do what's best. And you can count on him for doing it too. Yes, sir.'

Lifting Buck's nose gently, the straight edge took the last of the cream from his upper lip. Using the towel to wipe his customer's face, the barber removed the cloth cover.

'There you go, young man. Now then,' he said turning to Louie, 'are you next?'

Louie shook his head. 'No, thank you. I don't feel comfortable having someone getting that close to me with a weapon like that.'

Buck, laughing, paid the barber. 'So what times are you talking about, exactly, when the sheriff does his job?'

'Wal, there's two kinds calling for Mac to do the right thing. Take for instance when a fella comes out of the saloon, say on a Saturday night, having taken on too much liquor. He's celebrating something, let's say, and starts shooting up the sky. Well, that's when Mac does his job and carefully removes the fella before any real damage is done. Spending the night in the jail is a good way to control that. Then there's the occasion when after selling a herd, the hands let off steam. They could also be celebrating but somehow it's a different matter. That's when ol' Mac uses his head and goes fishing.'

'Goes fishing?'

'Yes sir. You see Mac knows when such an event is gonna happen. Or is most likely to take place. So before things get too out of hand he loads his saddlebags up with fishing pole and the like and goes down to the river. It's only a couple miles to his favourite fishing hole down there. The next day, after the cowboys have all gone back to the ranch he comes back into town and finds everything peaceful. Knowing how to handle each kind of incident is what makes Mac a good sheriff.'

Buck glanced at Louie and nodded.

'Yeah,' he said, settling his hat and heading for the shop's door, 'I can see what you mean. Uh huh. I surely do.'

Out on the street the pair stopped. 'Well, compadre,' said Louie quietly, 'do you think the town's good sheriff would have anything to tell us that'd be helpful?'

'Got to start somewhere. Personally I don't feel like riding blindly out and about. Yeah, let's see what the sheriff has to say.'

From the barber shop down to the sheriff's office didn't take long. Traffic along the street was light, only a couple of wagons moving along and no more than a rider or two. No more than a handful of horses were standing head down, dozing at a few of the hitchrails. This was typical, Buck thought, for a middle-of-the-week day in any of a hundred towns this size. Or even a thousand. Saturday was when the most business was done, when folks from the outlying ranches and farms came in to shop. Whole families making the trip an occasion.

Opening the door and stepping inside, Buck quickly saw all there was to see. The man sitting behind a spur-marked desk looked to have been dozing, waking up with a start. On the wall behind was a rack holding a half-dozen or so rifles and shotguns.

Along the far side, bound by a lattice-work of strap iron was a single jail cell.

'Hurmph,' the man, obviously the sheriff, snorted abruptly coming awake. 'Wal, now, what can I do for you?' Frowning and quickly studying the two men he nodded, 'Oh, yes, you'd be the men they've hired. Uh huh. I been expecting you. Come on in and take a chair,' motioning to spindle-backed chairs sitting in front of his desk. 'How about a cup of coffee while we talk? Was from this morning but I reckon its still drinkable.'

Buck glanced back toward a black iron stove, nodded and went over to pick up the pot sitting on top. Taking cups to the desk he poured into two of them and then filled the near empty cup sitting in front of the sheriff.

'Yes,' he said sitting down, 'I'm Buck Armstrong and this is my partner, Louie Lewis. And yes, we're the men they hired. Guess if anyone in town can tell us anything about this Vigilance

Committee it'd be you.'

'Naw, there's not much I can tell you. Except they've been damn busy. Whoever they are, there's been six or seven men stretched and left hanging. Now mostly people wouldn't care too much, if all of them were really rustlers. But in at least one case it don't seem likely.'

'What made that one questionable?'

'The fella hung up had come into town a few days earlier. Got hisself a room at the hotel even. Didn't say much to anyone, was last seen riding out. Minding his own business. Didn't come back and when a couple kids came busting in yelling and carrying on it was clear why. They had spotted him hanging from a tree limb beside the road. Scared 'em a mite, I'd say.'

'And the Committee had pinned a sign on him?'

'Sure did. Don't know how they came by the idea, but it didn't seem to matter.'

Buck sipped the coffee. The sheriff was right, it was drinkable, but only barely. 'And the others? Were they all for sure rustlers?'

'No way of knowing, is there? Unless you catch them in the act of changing brands or running off someone's cattle there ain't too many ways to prove they're outlaws. But in each case, excepting the one, the hanging took place close by where cattle were.'

'We've been told there are two big ranches and a few smaller spreads in this part of the territory. Could anyone from these places be part of this Committee?'

'Again, don't know for sure. It's likely. I mean not everyone is against what that bunch is doing. Some folks think it's a good thing. The ranches are what keeps Auburn alive so anything that hurts the ranches, hurts the town.'

Buck tried to think of questions he could ask in order to get a place to start.

'What caused this Vigilance Committee to start in? Has there been an increase in rustling in this area?'

'Can't say what's behind it. And from what I hear not all the ranches are suffering from any rustling, either. I'd guess the Frying Pan and Runkle's are the big losers but then most of their cattle are spread out on the open range. Seems to me with only a few roving hands to protect them they'd be most likely the ones to show up missing stock. But I'm just a small-town lawman. I don't know too much about such things.'

Louie had been listening. 'Yes, your mayor warned us not everyone wants to see the Committee stopped. But having the hangings reported in the newspapers is not good for the territory. Something to do with statehood.'

'Uh huh. That there's something fairly new for Auburn, and for the territory itself. The push to become a state. Both the idea of statehood and the Vigilance Committee. All coming at about the same time. Makes you wonder, doesn't it?'

6

Buck's first opinion on the town lawman was slowly changing. Sheriff McDonald wasn't the sleepy, bluff kind of man simply holding down a do-nothing job as he first appeared to be.

Sitting behind the desk it was difficult to see much about him, except for the rounded shoulders and broad chest. Buck figured him to be about fifty and probably overweight. Again it was hard to tell, the sheriff's black leather vest worn over a denim blue shirt pretty well hid things. The skin from his neck up looked evenly tanned, and being mostly bald, there was a lot of skin to see. A frizzy hedge of thin grey hair circled above his ears.

It was the man's eyes that told the most; clear, blue eyes with a steady gaze as he talked about the vigilantes.

'One of the most vocal of the ranchers is Fitzwalter. Henry Raymond Fitzwalter. He's a funny duck. Has a piece of range out at the foot of the Waller Mountains. That's what the mountains over east of here are called. The Wallers aren't all that high but they make a clear boundary between our side of the territory and the more populated side. Now over there is where folks have more problems. That's the main reason, I'd say, we don't see much of the federal marshal; he's busy trying to keep the peace.'

'Why's that?' asked Louie. 'How come there's so much law trouble over there?'

'Well, first off the territorial governor is there and that means all the territorial government. But the real problem is caused by outlaws and other low-class baddies escaping Texas and Oklahoma. Too many running for safety in the territory after committing crimes. We haven't the big banks carrying lots of money like in those places. Now here, in our little town, I'm able to keep a pretty good handle on things, but that only makes it possible for gangs like this Vigilance Committee to be possible. Or as some think, necessary.'

'The Vigilance Committee,' said Buck, wanting to get back to it, 'who else would you say are supporting them? Other ranchers than this Fitzwalter you mentioned?'

'Well, Runkle says he has the men to protect his interests and don't need or want any bunch of vigilantes running around. Jacobson, he isn't so sure the Committee is a good thing. He don't talk much and I don't know if he's losing stock to rustlers. No, the main one applauding the vigilantes would be Fitz.'

'What kind of spread does he have?' asked Buck.

'Well, he supplies horses for the big boys. Got himself a section when the homesteader who filed on the land was shot. Nate Price was his name. Set himself up, built a pretty good little operation raising horses and breaking them to saddle. About a year, or maybe two, um, yeah, two years ago his body was found. He'd been shot in the back. I went out and looked around. Couldn't find anything and nobody was ever charged. Anyway a short time later Fitz came in, looked the place over and bought the 160 acres from the government. Paid twenty dollars an acre, he did.

'Hired himself a foreman and a couple hands and went back to dealing with horses. Stays pretty much to himself out there. Don't come into town much. But has made his feelings about the vigilantes clear.'

Thinking about it, Buck finally nodded. Standing up, he reached across to shake the sheriff's hand. 'Well, Sheriff,' he said, 'I guess we've got our work cut out for us. I do thank you for your time and we'll keep you informed if we do find anything worthwhile.'

Starting for the door, he stopped and

turned back. 'You say the federal marshal doesn't come over very often. How often is that?'

Sheriff McDonald chuckled. 'Only as often as I telegraph him, yelling for help. Which means not often.'

Buck smiled and went out. Thinking about what the sheriff had told them, Buck and Louie decided to go have a beer and talk.

The same bartender was behind the long bar, still polishing glasses. Looking up as the two men came through the doors, he frowned.

'There ain't no one in here today for you to chase out. I certainly hope that isn't going to happen often. It ain't like there's so many customers coming in I can afford to lose even one.'

Buck laughed. 'Nope. We're here this afternoon as customers. Just a nice quiet beer nearing the end of a hard working day.'

Sitting at one of the smaller tables with a pitcher of beer in front of them, they relaxed.

'Guess the next thing,' said Buck after sipping his beer, 'is to go over to the hotel and get a room. I don't know what we've accomplished since riding into town but I'm looking forward to a good night's sleep.'

Louie nodded. 'And another meal one of us don't have to cook. But do you think we learned anything worthwhile today? I mean other than having that beautiful young woman try to run us down out in the street?'

Buck chuckled. 'I don't know. Nobody seems to have any idea who is part of this so-called Committee. What interests me is how there are folks against them and others in favour of what they're doing. You'd think everybody would be up in arms about a gang going around hanging men, without having a trial even. And apparently, in a couple cases, possibly not actual rustlers.'

Their talk halted when a man came striding into the long room. Looking over at the newcomer, Buck frowned.

There was something familiar about the man.

For a moment the man stood letting his eyes adjust as he scanned the room. Not giving the bar-tender more than a glance, he focused directly on the two sitting to one side. There was no expression on his face as he seemed to study Buck and Louie. Then nodding as if in agreement he strode with almost military precision to their table.

'Buck Armstrong and Louie Lewis. You're just who I'm looking for,' said the man, standing unsmiling, looking down at the pair. 'My name is Yarberry, Harry Yarberry. I've been hired to stop you.' Holding up a hand to halt either man from reacting he quickly went on. 'Understand me, there is nothing personal in this. Just like you I'm merely doing what I am paid to do. About the vigilantes, I don't care one way or another. Probably best to just let things work themselves out. And I've got nothing against either of you. My job is to stop you from meddling. Now

51

this is the only warning you'll get. Ride out now and that'll be the end of it. Go on with what you're doing and I'll kill you. Both of you.'

Making eye contact with each man one at a time, Yarberry nodded, turned, and as if on a parade ground, marched out the door.

7

There was a silence, somehow thick and still, in the saloon after the man had gone. Finally after a long moment, Louie broke the quiet.

'Did that really happen? We just sat there and let him tell us he was going to kill us?'

Buck nodded. 'Yeah. I guess he did. Kinda caught us unexpectedly, didn't he?'

'I'll say. Yarberry. You know, I somehow . . . it's almost like I'd heard it before. Yarberry.'

'Harry Yarberry,' said Buck, frowning. 'It was probably before you joined the Rangers. I'd only been wearing the star myself a short time. But even then, stories of Harry Yarberry was being told. Likely that's why the name is almost familiar to you.'

'Maybe so. He's a cold-looking dude, isn't he?'

'A killer. Got him kicked out of the Rangers, his willingness to kill people. Not much was ever proved, though. Even though most everybody knew what'd happened.'

'What did happen?' asked the bartender standing as close as he could but still remain behind the bar. 'That fella didn't look one way or the other, just came in and walked over to you and, bang. Said his piece and walked out. Not a care in the world. You knew him?'

Buck glanced over at the barkeep and nodded. 'I probably met him at one time or another. It'd be when I was pretty new and was still learning about being a Texas Ranger. The stories floating around later were everywhere. Seemed everyone had something to say about the man. I don't know. I was busy thinking about other things. That'd be about when the war with Mexico ended. Or soon after. About that time the US government was making Texas a full and official state. There was some rush to get it done. Probably had something to do with the slave issue. I wasn't paying much attention.'

'He got kicked out, though?' the bartender asked.

'Yeah. He was formally discharged from the Rangers after being suspected of shooting another fellow, Thomas Wilton by name. Yarberry had been taken into custody but the judge had to release him when the only witness to the shooting, Wilton's wife, declined to testify. As soon as Yarberry was let go he left that part of the state. That'd be down in Jack County, Texas. Yup, left behind the widow Wilton he did. Boy, was she mad. When she heard he was gone the widow hurried down to the marshal and claimed she'd been wrong. Said Yarberry had shot her husband and she wanted him arrested and retried in court.'

'Well, was he?' asked Louie, taken up by the story.

'No. As the man was gone from Texas

nothing was done.'

'And now,' said Louie, 'he's here in Auburn, threatening to kill us.'

'Uh huh. Seems that's what he's become, a paid killer.'

The bartender, wiping one spot on the bar, didn't want the story to end. 'He must have some history. What'd he do after leaving the Rangers?'

'Well, from what I heard he settled for a time up in Texarkana, Arkansas. Killed a man there. Guess he thought the fellow was a bounty hunter.'

'Was there a bounty on him?' asked Louie.

Buck chuckled. 'Uh huh. Two hundred dollars. It'd been put up by Marie Wilton, widow of Thomas Wilton. After shooting the man in Arkansas, Yarberry was next heard of in Decatur, Texas. He bought into a saloon there. However when a bounty hunter came to Decatur and started asking questions, Yarberry sold out and left town. It was a couple days later the bounty hunter's body was found just outside of town, shot dead.

'Story goes Yarberry went north and met up with a fellow named Johnny Preston. They opened a saloon in Las Vegas, New Mexico. About a year later the bartender shot and wounded Preston. Yarberry, said to be handy with a pistol, shot and killed the bartender. Well, he figured he'd better travel so he sold out to his partner, Preston, who was healing. Moving on he ran a brothel for a while, I forget where exactly, but left when they suspected he'd killed a man named John Morgan. That shooting was over a prostitute, according to the story I heard.'

'A killer for sure,' said the bartender, still wiping the bar.

'Yeah. He sold his share in the brothel and moved back to New Mexico. That's where his former partner, John Preston, still lived. Well, as it turned out Johnny caught Yarberry in bed with his wife, Sadie. Both men fired but Johnny missed. Yarberry didn't and Johnny was wounded again. The town sheriff tried to arrest Yarberry over that shooting but he'd disappeared leaving behind Sadie and Johnny, who died a short time later.'

'Lordy me,' said the bartender, 'is that when he started selling his gun?'

'I guess. Seems I heard he was hiring himself out for as little as $150.'

'Damn,' exclaimed Louie, 'I'd like to think either one of us was worth more than that.'

'Doesn't seem enough, does it? Someone certainly got a bargain. I got to wonder though, who hired him? Who don't want us doing what we're supposed to do?'

The bartender shook his head in disgust. 'You fellas live too dangerous a life for me. Think I'll just go on pouring whiskey and beer for y'all. A lot safer. Want another beer?'

'Well, barkeep,' said Louie, chuckling, 'I for one like all the fresh air I get doing what we do. It's what keeps us healthy. OK, Buck,' he turned to his partner, 'where do you reckon we go from here?'

'We have to know more about things. Let's go get that room, then have supper. Tomorrow morning will be soon enough to go asking questions. I suspect the best thing to do will be to find the mayor, see what he can tell us.'

8

The next morning, after a hearty breakfast of steak and eggs washed down with a pot of fresh boiled coffee, the two men set out to find more information about the local Vigilance Committee.

'I reckon the place to start,' said Buck, dropping a few coins on the table in the restaurant, 'will be with the mayor. He's the one who's going to end up paying us.'

Louie carefully wiped his hands on a napkin before using them to settle his Stetson just so. 'Seems likely,' he said, 'being mayor he'd know more what's going on than the barber or even the bartender.'

Buck started to nod in agreement but stopped. 'You know, there is one person who might know even more than anyone. I plumb forgot about the owner of the local newspaper.'

The newspaper office was around the corner from the hotel. Stepping in, the two were assailed by the odd odour.

'What's that? Something crawled under the floor and died?' Louie asked, turning up his nose.

'No sir,' came an answer from behind the counter that ran across the room. A young man wearing an ink-stained apron over an equally ink-stained shirt came up like a child's jack-in-the-box toy. 'It's just carbon black and a little linseed oil,' explained the man, his face lit by a big smile. 'Got a smell but hang around a while and you'll get used to it. Now then, what can I do for you two gentlemen?'

Standing next to him was another young man. In contrast he was clean and well-scrubbed.

'We're looking for the newspaper editor,' said Buck. 'Would like to ask him a few questions.'

'Yes sir, you're looking at him. Name's Toby Sinclair. Been editor, printer, paper deliver boy, floor sweeper and all-round answer man for the town of Auburn for the past nine months. This here is my friend, Jacob Bass. Doctor Jacob Bass. If I can't come up with an answer to your questions, old Jacob here can. So ask away.'

Buck laughed. 'Doctor Bass? Are you the town doctor?'

The two men looked to be about the same age. Buck's first thought was they might be brothers, the same build and the same intelligent look in their eyes. The major difference was one was dressed in clean and pressed shirt and pants and the other's clothes were blackened with ink.

'Yes,' answered the doctor, 'at least I'm the only one in town.'

'Well, it's good to know there is one somewhere close by. But Mr Sinclair, why only nine months?'

Sinclair's smile grew even bigger. 'First off, it's Toby, not mister anything. And nine months? Well, nine months is time enough to have a baby, if you're a woman in the family way. Or the time it took for me to get things organized after Pa died. He'd come out here to the territories a few years ago to set up the paper. It's a growing place, he said. Wanted to be in on that growth. I, on the other hand, stayed back in college. I started there at the end of the War, in Little Rock, Arkansas. I was quite happy, I'll tell you, until he died leaving me the paper and all its bills. So here I am, trying to make enough to feed me, my dog and the folks Pa owed money to. Now, what are your questions?'

'Well,' said Louie, 'after all that there ain't much we don't know, is there?'

Shaking his head, Buck smiled. 'We've been hired to do something about the gang calling themselves the Vigilance Committee. Been told some of the local folks think this gang is doing good work. One of your editorials was read to us but didn't name any names. So can you tell us who you think believes hanging rustlers is a good thing?'

'Ah, yes. I heard someone was coming to town to clean out this Committee. I'd like to interview you about that. Why you're doing this kind of work, how you're going to do what they hired you to do and what will you do when you catch some of the gang members. That would make a good story for the paper.'

Buck shook his head. 'Can't see how it would help us, telling the members of the Committee what we're doing. All we're trying to do is get a start on this Vigilance Committee. But can you answer our questions?'

'I for one don't think they are good for the area, so go ahead. I'll tell you what you want to know, if I can.'

Bass held up a hand. 'Wait a minute, gentlemen. If I may interrupt. I'm new to all this. Born, raised and educated in the big city. Now you're talking about vigilantes and rustlers. I have a general idea what those are but not more than that. Can you help me out here a little? What exactly are you talking about?'

Sinclair chuckled. 'Jason is the intellectual half of the team. We met at college. He was just getting his doctor programme completed when I had to come out to Auburn. We've been, well, kind of partners so, not having a practice, he decided to come with me.'

The doctor nodded. 'A chance to see a part of the country I've only ever heard about,' explained Bass. 'It's all brand new to us, and I must say, a little exciting. But there is so much we don't know. Toby is more familiar with a lot of it, more than I, and I apologize for being so inquisitive.'

Buck shook his head. 'No reason for it. I reckon things are a mite different out here. You have to understand, once you get away from the city you won't find many lawmen. Here in town you've got Sheriff McDonald. But there isn't much he can do outside the town's limits. Over at Fort Rawlins there's a federal territorial marshal, however he's got the whole territory to cover so there's not much he can do either.

Until something major happens. But he's still only one, or if he's got a deputy, maybe two men. That means out in the country the law is scarce. Louie and I were Texas Rangers. So we've had some experience. Cause of that, we've been hired by the folks here to put a halt to a gang calling themselves the Vigilance Committee.'

Bass nodded. 'And this Committee, they are stopping rustlers? Those being cattle thieves?'

'Yup. Again, you have to keep in mind there's a whole lot of open country out here. Prairies with few people. The livestock on most of the larger ranches simply roam around, feeding and getting fat. Oh, yeah, the hands will ride around during the year, checking the stock, cleaning waterholes and generally keeping an eye on things. That leaves a lot of country and a lot of cattle or horses that only get seen or tallied come round-up time. This makes it good pickings for someone wanting to steal another man's stock.'

'Back in Arkansas we'd have the police or possibly the Army to protect someone's livestock. I can see how that wouldn't work here. So this Committee is doing the lawman's work for them. What do these rustlers do? Simply drive the cattle or horses off?'

Buck nodded. 'Sometimes. Rustling can be done in a number of ways. Down in Texas there are thousands of head running wild. A fella might simply register his brand, hire hands to go out and round up as many as they can, put his brand on them. Those cattle then belong to him. Driven up north to the railhead he can make pretty good money. Now this isn't exactly rustling, branding wild stock. They're called mavericks. But not all cattle roaming out on open range are wild. Around here there's a couple big spreads with stock doing just that, roaming around putting on weight. So let's say a couple men come in, gather up a couple dozen head and walk them on out to the nearest rail road. That is another kind of rustling.

'You have to remember, the ranchers don't know exactly how many head they've got. But come round-up time, when they go to branding and getting a herd together for a drive, they can pretty much tell if they're missing stock. Oh, a few head here or there might not be missed, but rustlers can't make money by taking only a few head. It's when the rustling gets too big that something must be done. The sheriff can't go chasing around and the marshal can't either. The territory is just too big. That's when, often, to protect themselves the ranchers will get together and try to catch the rustlers. We were hired because the problem here is with a gang who not only hang rustlers but have strung up a few men who might not be thieves.'

'And now you've got the job. How can you catch them? I mean, you would have to be lucky to find them hanging someone, wouldn't you?'

'Yeah. Unless someone knows something that'll help us identify who's on this Committee, they'll be hard to stop. That's what we're hoping Mr Sinclair, uh, Toby, can help us with.' Turning to the newspaper man, he smiled. 'That's our question; do you have any idea who is on the Committee?' When Sinclair shook his head, Buck went on, 'How about who is all for the vigilantes?'

'I still say it don't seem fair,' said Sinclair, 'you're wanting information but not willing to give me any. However I can see your point. All right. Let's see, top of the list I'd say would be the big ranchers, Jacobson and Runkle. Those two just about run things around here. Then there's Fitzwalter, he's always talking about the good work the Committee is doing. A couple owners of businesses here in Auburn seem to like the Committee too. I can't quite figure that out. Hmm, I'd say those were the main ones.'

'Well, that gives us a couple names of people to talk to, a place to start.'

'Glad I'm able to help. Tell you what, anything else I hear I'll pass on to y'all. In trade, once you're finished you'll come in and let me interview you. Does that sound fair?'

Both Louie and Buck laughed and nodded their agreement.

9

Finding Mayor Winterbottom wasn't difficult. Turned out he owned the town's only general store. The first thing striking Buck when he walked into the store was the odour; an odd mixture of leather from the delicately carved high-cantled saddles on a rack near the door to the sugary-sweet aroma wafting up from a large barrel of colourful hard candies. Standing behind the counter beyond the barrel was an attractive young woman.

More closely a girl rather than a woman, Buck figured she looked to be about twenty. Her face was framed by golden blonde hair hanging in long curls to the shoulders of her pale blue full-bosomed dress. The young woman's eyes sparkled as she was softly laughing.

'Good morning gentlemen,' she said,

smiling from ear to ear.

Louie frowned. 'What's so funny? I buttoned my shirt crooked or something?'

She appeared to be barely able to contain herself. 'Forgive me, but I've been wondering what the two of you would say when you came in.'

'You knew we'd be in?' asked Louie, glancing sideways at Buck.

'Oh, I figured sooner or later you'd want to talk to my father.'

Buck nodded. 'But what is so funny about that?'

'Well, nothing. What I was thinking about was how you'd likely react when you found out where Rose Marie was heading when she almost ran you down yesterday.'

'I can't hardly see,' said Louie starting to let his anger show, 'how being run down in the street would be funny.'

'No, and I am sorry for laughing. But when Rose told me, well, we started laughing and almost couldn't stop. But you're correct, it wasn't funny. To you, anyway. You see, Rose is always like that; rushing from here to there. And she thinks because she's Mr Jacobson's only daughter it makes her someone special. Being the unmarried daughter of the wealthiest man in the area and having every single man in fifty miles sniffing around does that, I guess.'

Neither man saw anything comical in what the young woman was saying. 'From what she said as she barrelled by us,' said Buck seriously, 'she had somewhere important to go. What was she late for, anyway?'

'That's what was so funny. She was coming here, to see me. That's all. We get together every so often, to gossip and talk about the men who've found reason to visit the Frying Pan.'

Still serious, Buck frowned. 'Can't speak for Louie here, but I fail to see how funny and exciting that must have been. But never mind, you're correct. We are here to talk with Mayor Winterbottom. Is he anywhere around?'

Suddenly sober, the woman looked from one man to the other. 'Oh, yes, he's back there,' she pointed toward the rear of the store, 'doing some paper-work.'

Without another word the two men walked back and found the round-shouldered man hunched over a desk, studying a newspaper.

10

William Winterbottom, mayor of Auburn and owner of the town's general store, hadn't always been the mayor. His family had once owned a cotton farm on the Brazos River in the old Republic of Texas. The family originally came from England, emigrating when they learnt of the availability of good farm land. With the use of Mexican farm labour, the Winterbottom cotton farms were very successful. When the southern states seceded from the north, the bottom fell out of the cotton industry.

The youngest of four boys, when the last farm was declared bankrupt by the banks, William left the family. For a few years he worked on farms farther north and even at one point a cattle ranch. It was in Fort Worth he became a clerk in a clothing store. Life in the big city was good. When he married the store owner's daughter, Tilly, it got even better. Until giving birth to their first child. Complications set in and while the newborn daughter was healthy, squalling so, the mother died.

Taking his daughter, Mathilda, or Matty as she was called growing up, William left Fort Worth. Matty was just reaching womanhood when they got off the stage in Auburn, up in the Indian Territory.

'Raising a daughter by yourself,' he was heard to say at the time, 'and hoping she'll grow up to be a lady like her mother was is one of the hardest jobs a man can take on.'

Arriving in Auburn with just enough money to buy the town's only general store, the Winterbottoms put down roots. Actually, it was Mathilda who put her foot down.

'We've been moving from place to place, Pa,' she said in a voice that brooked no argument, 'and it's time to settle. It would have been better back in one of the bigger towns but Auburn will have to do.'

Being one of the handful of business owners in town made William a big fish in a little pond. When the town's mayor died, having been bit by a rattlesnake, William put his hand up and was quickly accepted.

Over the next few years Matty developed into being a very attractive young woman. Not, it was true, as pretty as her friend Rose Marie Jacobson, but in a country with few unmarried women, attractive enough to have many suitors.

'I look forward to the day my daughter accepts the notion of marriage,' William remarked one afternoon to the town barber while getting his hair cut. Over the years William hadn't missed many meals. Not being a big man to start with, and enjoying the beer brewed by the owner of the nearest saloon, he found himself almost regularly taking wool pants with bigger and bigger waists from the shelf. His visits to the barber became farther apart too, as his hair got thinner and thinner. But through it all, becoming bald, getting rounder shouldered and worrying about his daughter, he was able to keep a happy outlook.

'Yes,' he told the bartender, a man almost as round-bellied as he was, 'having an unmarried daughter in the house does pose problems. Now, it isn't her fault, no sir,' he paused, then went on, 'well, not really. Uh huh. It's the men who come into the store. Not to make a purchase but to talk with Matty. Of course she likes it, but, well, you know. You got any children?' When the bartender shook his head, William nodded. 'Then you won't understand what I have to go through. Sure wish she'd settle down and get hitched.'

11

'Mayor Winterbottom,' said Buck quietly, 'don't want to bother you but we've got a couple questions.'

Winterbottom looked up, grimacing. 'Have you seen the latest edition of the papers? This one comes over from Fort Rawlins. Dropped off by the morning stage. Here it is, front page, more about the vigilantes over here. Why would that be news to anyone over on that side of the mountains? I ask you. This is the kind of thing I was telling you about. Stories like this don't sit well with those fools in Congress. Not when we're trying to convince them we're settled enough to become a state. Oh, damn!' he exclaimed, bunching up the paper and throwing it to the floor.

'Well,' said Buck calmly, 'if we can get a few answers maybe we can get busy and do something about that.'

'Oh, yes,' said Winterbottom, calming down. 'I'm sorry to get so upset. But it riles me to no end.' Taking a deep breath he glanced first at Buck then the other man. 'All right, what can I tell you that'll help?'

'First off, you mentioned thinking some of those helping put up the money to hire us don't exactly see the negatives of the vigilantes. Can you tell us who that would be?'

'Uh huh. Easy. Both Handley Runkle and Carl Jacobson put up the most money and both made it clear they thought it was a waste of time. Whoever they are, those calling themselves the Vigilance Committee, what they're doing is good according to the two ranchers. Neither thinks they're losing many head to rustlers. They don't seem to understand what it means to the statehood proposal.'

'Anyone else? Did these two put up all the money by themselves?'

'Well, no. Fitzwalter added a little, and so did most of the business owners here in town. As mayor I felt I had to give even more. Both as mayor and owner of the store.'

'This Fitzwalter, Sheriff McDonald and the editor of the local paper seemed to think he was one of the strongest supporters of the Committee. What's his story?'

'Oh, I don't really know much about him. Doesn't come into town all that much. Stays pretty close to the home ranch.'

'Yeah, McDonald says he just recently bought the range home-steaded by a man who was killed. Can you tell us anything about that?'

'Naw, just what people were saying. Happened out a couple miles from his main house. The ranch was put together by a fella named Price. Got hisself a good little herd of range horses, mustangs ya know. Called his spread the Mustang Ranch. Out there close to the mouth of the valley. Last spread up against the foothills. Found his body lying in the road. Fitz comes along a while later, having bought Price's holdings. He goes on buying and selling horses, you know. Hired hisself a foreman who knows about horses. Fitz goes out on buying trips and comes back with a slew of half-wild stock. The foreman and a couple hands then work the animals into some kind of shape, saddle breaks them, you know. Sells most of that stock to Jacobson and Runkle. To look at Fitz you'd think he was straight out of the city. Wears city suits, not jeans and pointy-toed riding boots like most men around here do. Can't tell you much more'n that. He don't usually say too much. Just listens and then nods or shakes his head. Strange fellow.'

Back on the street, after walking past the young woman at the front counter without saying anything, the two men stood for a moment.

'Guess the next thing to do,' said Buck, pulling gently at his hat brim, getting it comfortable, 'is to go talk a bit with the big spenders. I'm guessing our best way to finding out anything about this Committee will be to let those fellows come to us. If we start digging, I'll bet it won't take long for someone in that gang to come calling. Maybe sending Yarberry to do his work. I don't know, but if we can't find them, let them come find us.'

Louie frowned and looking up and down the street, nodded.

'Can't think of any other way to get the ball rolling. But, partner, we'll have to keep our eyes open. If that Yarberry does come calling, we better be ready.'

'Probably goes for anyone in that Vigilance Committee, too.'

12

Buck's stud horse didn't like it much when he threw a saddle on, inhaling and puffing up his belly when Buck went to buckling up the cinch strap. Buck chuckled and jamming a knee into the horse's side, jerked the strap tight.

'Damn fool horse. Give you a bit of freedom in the corral and you get stupid.'

Louie, busy saddling his own horse, laughed. 'Seems like your black horse would learn. He tries that about every time.'

'Oh, he's smart enough. Just thinks he's smarter than me and has to be shown it isn't true.'

Being careful of the big teeth, Buck slipped the bit into the animal's mouth and stepping into the saddle, swung aboard. 'Guess we ought to stop by the sheriff's office. Been so busy listening to people tell what little they know about the Committee, I never found out which way it is to Jacobson's spread.'

Stopping in front of the office, Buck was about to swing down when a horse came galloping down the dirt street. Bouncing in the saddle on the big, dapple grey horse was a boy about ten or so.

'Sheriff, Sheriff,' yelled out the youngster, hauling back on the reins and jumping to the ground. 'Sheriff, there's a man hangin' from the bridge down by the river. Ya gotta come.'

Before the boy could get to the office door it came open and Sheriff McDonald came out tucking in his shirttail. 'Hey there, Freddie. Slow down and stop yelling. Now, take a deep breath and tell me what the excitement is all about.'

The boy stopped and did what he was told; standing still and looking down, inhaled. Holding it for a moment, he looked up, exhaled and started in again. 'There's a man hangin' from the bridge,' he said patiently. 'Ya gotta come see.'

Turning back toward his horse he stopped when the sheriff put a hand on his shoulder. 'Now let's wait a minute. If there's someone hanging as you say, he isn't going anywhere soon.' Glancing up at Buck and Louie, he smiled. 'Now, Freddie, take your time and tell us what you saw. What are you doing coming into town so early in the morning, anyhow?'

'I was coming into town when I saw him,' said Freddie, slowing down as he explained. 'Had a list of things Ma wanted from the store and couldn't wait till Saturday to come get. Left home early so I could stop down there where the bridge over the river is. Good fishing right there and, well, I don't get away from my chores too often, ya know. Anyway I was hurrying old Homer here, he's getting on and don't like to go faster than a walk. But I was pushing him so I'd have plenty of time to fish. It was after sun-up but likely before the store was opened.

'Y'all know that stretch of scrub trees on the far side of the bridge? The road through those woods twists around a bit between the trees and I was gigging old Homer along and wasn't paying no mind to anything else. When we came outa the trees old Homer shied a bit off to one side and stopped. I was about to jab him in the ribs when I looked up and there the man was, hangin' off the side of the bridge, his feet just about dippin' in the water.'

'Could you see who it was?' asked Sheriff McDonald.

'Nope. His face was all purpled up and kinda hanging off to one side. Didn't look like anyone from around here. Nobody I'd ever seen before.' Glancing at the folks listening to what he had to say, he squared his shoulders and, trying to sound grown-up, nodded like he'd seen his pa do. 'I reckon it was someone caught stealing horses or something. Pa says them what goes taking livestock what don't belong to them should oughta get hung. That's what Pa says.'

McDonald turned to where Buck and Louie were sitting. 'Most likely the work of the Vigilance Committee. Probably letting you two know they aren't afraid of you. Well,' he motioned to the boy, 'y'all go on over to the store and get what your ma sent you for. I'll go get a wagon and ride out to the bridge. It probably isn't a good thing for a youngster like yourself to be seeing such things.'

13

It was just as Freddie described. The man, the bottom of his worn canvas pants dripping wet, was swinging from a rope tied to the side of the log bridge.

It didn't take them long to get the body down and laid out on the bank of the slow moving river.

'Nope,' said the sheriff after taking a long look at the body, 'isn't anyone I've ever seen before. From the looks of him, his clothes are all dusty and all, I'd say he's likely been travelling.'

'A cowhand, I'd say,' said Buck, pointing to the dead man's boots. 'No gun belt but his pants are worn like he usually had one. No hat either. Bet when you look in his pockets you won't find much of anything. I'll bet who ever hung him up took everything.'

Louie climbed up on the bridge and stood taking a long look around.

'Sheriff, this is the road out to the big ranches, isn't it? Well, I'll make my own bet. Buck, bet you fifty cents this gent was hung up by someone knowing we'd be riding this way. They wanted to make sure we got their message. Can't see if anyone's been watching to make sure. Could be a small army hidden back in that bunch of trees over there.'

'Hmm, you could be right. And if so, well, they succeeded — we got the message. Too bad for this gent, though.'

'This isn't going to stop you, is it?' asked the sheriff.

'Nope. It don't change anything. Louie and me, well, we haven't been paid yet, but now I'd say we got a more personal reason to put an end to this. If the Committee is going to go killing men, trying to warn us off, our message is it isn't going to work.'

14

Leaving the body to the sheriff, Buck and Louie rode on. According to the directions Sheriff McDonald gave them, the stage road north out of Auburn wound around passing by most of the ranches in the valley. Louie wasn't as calm as he appeared. Seeing a fella hanging from the bridge and being sure someone was watching made him a little nervous.

He'd been riding alongside Buck Armstrong for quite a while. Long before they left the Rangers. He'd been there the day Buck defied Sergeant Healy. The Sergeant had led the Dunn's Fort detachment ever since the war over slavery ended. Story goes he'd been one of the early volunteers signing onto the Rangers about the time Texas cut away from Mexico.

A strong-willed man, Healy's reputation was one most Rangers looked up to. He'd fought in the US-Mexican war and then when Rangers were given the job of cleaning up the Indian troubles, he fitted right in. For a long time warriors from both tribes, Apache and Comanche, had ravaged settlements, stealing cattle and killing whites. It took the US Army and the Rangers a long time to get control of things. Healy came out of it with nothing good to say about any Indian. Or any Mexican, for that matter.

The problem Buck stepped in was over a Mexican *vaquero*. Feliz Lopez y Gonzalez had been one of the best horsemen in the area. Ranchers had brought their rough strings to him for saddle-breaking for at least a half-dozen years. Feliz had a reputation for doing a good job. When he delivered a string of ten mustangs to the city corral, was when things fell apart. According to Feliz, the owner of the horses, a German rancher named August Hertzog had offered him his usual fee when he took on the job.

Feliz had a new girlfriend, a pretty young woman living in Mex town. He had seen a beautiful spirited filly, a pinto, at Hertzog's ranch when he went to gather up the mustangs. Rather than the money, Feliz offered to do the work on Hertzog's horses in trade for the pinto. Witnesses said later Hertzog had agreed.

When Feliz delivered the string to the city corrals, as he was supposed to, Hertzog pointed to a broken-down old mare.

'That's yours now. We're even.'

Feliz shook his head. 'No, *señor*, that is not the pinto we agreed on.'

'Well, Mex, that's the horse you're getting. Take it and be damn glad you're getting that much.'

Feliz looked around and saw only white faces. Turning away, and ignoring Hertzog's laughter, he walked over to the Rangers' office. Explaining what had happened, Sergeant Healy frowned.

'You sure you're telling it like it was? I know that German, he can be ornery.

But far as I know he's always been fair. You musta made a mistake.'

Feliz didn't argue. Simply turning away, he climbed onto his horse and rode home.

A few days later Hertzog came into town and went straight to the Rangers' office. There he told Healy someone had stolen a young filly from his corral. Buck Armstrong was given the job of bringing in Feliz.

'And if he puts up a fight,' said Healy, 'go ahead and shoot him. It'll teach those damn Mexicans a lesson. It'd save us from having to hang him.'

Louie, a distant cousin of Feliz, told Buck about the men who had said they witnessed the deal the horse-breaker had made with Hertzog. Buck hunted up the men and heard again how it had happened. Taking it back to Healy, Buck said he didn't think bringing in Feliz was right.

Healy hadn't gotten along with Buck in the past and when he argued, the Sergeant saw a way to get rid of him.

Buck was fired. Louie, standing along-side Buck while he talked, tossed his badge onto Healy's desk alongside Buck's.

The two men rode out together and found out later Feliz had been brought in and judged guilty and was hung. It was after the hanging was near forgotten that Hertzog was seen selling the little pinto to a man travelling though the area.

Louie kept scanning the land around as they rode on out to the Frying Pan ranch.

'Hell, I can't get rid of the feeling we're being watched.'

Buck reached out and scratched the head of his black stud horse. 'Maybe. But I reckon Ol' Horse here will let us know if anyone comes out of the brush. He don't like other boy horses and loves getting close to any and all girl horses.'

Louie laughed and started relaxing.

The stage road, in places not much more than a pair of wagon-ruts cutting into the sod, stretched out through some of the best graze land Louie thought he'd ever seen. Unlike the dryness of back in town, the grass they rode through was good green cover. The only cattle they saw were in the far distance, so far away they couldn't tell if the animals were long-horns or Hereford short horns.

'Good-looking country for cattle,' said the man. Louie had grown up on his pa's cattle ranch, leaving only when tiring of the hard work and looking for adventure. Joining the Rangers gave him all that and more. 'Pa did a good job, raising cattle and selling his herds to some of the bigger outfits when they was making up to take a drive north. Guess he's still back there, doing what he'd always done. Boy, he'd certainly like a piece of this land.'

Buck, slowly rolling a smoke, nodded. 'Yeah, and that's likely the problem here. A few ranchers wanting to hold on to what they got and are afraid homesteaders will come in and take it.'

'Maybe,' said Louie, 'I just hope we don't get caught crosswise in this situation. I'm still thinking of that man, Yarberry. And don't forget Isaac Black. This little job we're supposed to do has some real chances for getting ourselves hurt bad.'

The high arched gate over the entrance to the Frying Pan ranch had been built of stone, curving up high and wide. Low stone walls angled off for a short way on either side. A huge plank sign hanging from the arch had the ranch name burned in big letters. The two went under the arch and rode another couple miles before seeing the main ranch buildings. They stopped when it came into view, looking it over. The ranch was a prime-looking outfit. A series of big, well-built barns sat off to one side of the road. Corrals, feed stalls and water barrels were strung out taking care of a herd of short-horned beeves, all looking well-fed and market ready. The big house at the end of the well-trod roadway had been built of peeled logs, all left natural setting off the white window frames. Shadow from verandas across the wide front looked cool and inviting.

A small group of men leaning on the railing of a corral turned to watch Buck and Louie ride in. The two stopped just before the men, staying in the saddle and keeping both hands folded on saddle horns. This didn't bother Louie. He'd been riding with Buck long enough; he knew his partner might look relaxed but if need be, was actually capable of reacting awfully sudden.

'You boys looking for something?' one of the men asked, not smiling. A slender man, slouching while standing a step away from the others. Louie, slowly moving his hand, thumbed the thong off his six-gun's hammer and kept his smile to himself. The man asking the question wore a holstered six-gun low on his thigh, within easy reach of his right hand. A would-be gun fighter,

Louie thought. The belt guns the other men wore were higher, tucked in high up on their hips. This was how most cowboys carried their pistols, out of the way and not likely to get snagged on anything. If any gunplay was to happen, he knew Buck would take out the fast gun first.

Typical of hired hands on every ranch, most of the men were wearing a variety of once-colorful denim shirts, all sun-bleached and looking faded. Wide-brimmed hats shaded their eyes: eyes watching and waiting. Only the gun fighter was wearing a black wool vest and had a brightly colored bandana tied around his neck. Since the pair rode up, none of the hands had changed their relaxed leaning against the corral poles.

While they were being studied, both Buck and Louie had been taking in the men and their surroundings. If asked, Louie decided this was about the best-looking operation he'd ever seen. All the buildings were well-kept and not needing paint. All of the corral poles were straight and strong. Even the yard in front of the main house appeared to have been swept. No weeds or grass were growing anywhere they shouldn't.

'Yeah, we are,' said Buck finally. 'Wanting to talk with the owner, Mr Jacobson.'

'What about?'

'Oh, I guess we'll talk with Jacobson about that.'

'Ah, hell, Smokey,' smirked another of the lazing men, 'you know who these jaspers are. They's here to put an end to the vigilantes.' He laughed. 'Although they may have a bit of trouble doing that, I figure.'

Buck smiled and pulling the makings from a shirt pocket, rolled a quirley. 'You say that, you must know something we don't. Something about who's on this so-called Committee? Wouldn't mind hearing about it.'

'Nope,' said the young man, 'I don't have anything to tell you. Exceptin' it ain't gonna be as easy as y'all think it'll be. Hear tell them what's on the

Vigilance Committee are meaner than any second-rate ex-Texas Rangers.'

Buck ignored the men as he scraped a kitchen match against his pants leg and lit his smoke. Finally glancing back at the men, he nodded. 'Well, I guess we'll see, won't we? Now, can you tell us if Mr Jacobson's at home?'

One of the men, slowly glancing right and left at the others, nodded. 'Guess you'll have to go knock on the door yourselves. Was I you, probably be best if y'all went around to the back door, though. You know, the servants' door.'

Louie chuckled as he and Buck reined their horses around and walked them toward the front.

'Boy,' Louie said as they climbed out of the saddle, 'not a lot of friendliness in that bunch.'

'Nope. They didn't make us feel at home, but then they didn't shoot us either. Somehow I wouldn't have been surprised if they had. C'mon, let's go see what the boss-man has to say.'

15

The man answering their knock was stockily built, looking to be in his late forties with crinkles around his deep-set eyes. For a moment he stood in the open doorway chuckling, holding the large heavy-looking door open, a slab of wood that had been decorated with carved curlicues.

'Come in, come in.' He stepped aside to let the pair through. 'Welcome to the Frying Pan,' the man said, shaking first one hand and then the other. 'I'm Carl Jacobson and you have got to be Armstrong and Lewis. I wondered how long it'd take you to get here. Yeah, I know who you are. Winterbottom told me he'd hired you last time I was in town. Here,' he motioned toward a couple brown leather easy chairs, 'let's get comfortable and talk a bit. I saw y'all ride in and figured you'd make your way up here to the house pretty quick so I asked Mirella to make us up a pot of coffee. She's my housekeeper. And cook and a whole lot of things ain't none of your business.'

Sitting down, Louie felt like he'd almost sunk into the softness. Looking around, he saw how big the room was. More of the heavy leather-covered sofas and easy chairs were scattered around than he'd ever seen outside of a big city hotel lobby. A large wood table sat along one wall, all smooth and polished to a slick sheen. Most of the far wall was taken up by a big fireplace, big enough to cook a small steer in. High overhead log rafters were barely visible in the shadows. Trying to decide whether he liked it or not, he looked up when a woman came into the room carrying a ceramic coffee pot and cups on a tray.

'*Señors*,' she said, smiling, and placed the tray on a small table in front of the chair the cattleman had taken. Flashing another smile at the men, she turned and hurried out of the room.

Carl Jacobson had been working for a ranch in Greer County, Texas when as a hired hand driving a herd of longhorns north to market, he came through this area. He took one look and knew he'd found what he had been looking for. To make the drive he'd left his 10-year-old daughter, Rose Marie, named after her mother, with the wife of another hand working the ranch.

It was a fact; cattle could be moved only a few miles a day. Push them faster than a walk and they would end up at the railhead thin and bony. The contrary beasts just had to eat along the way. Carl, a well-built young man in his early twenties, was a happy man. A good hand and well liked by the other hands, he was a very positive-minded person. When others cursed and yelled at one of the big horned beasts when deciding to walk away from the herd, Carl simply used his big chestnut quarter horse to round up the wandering animal.

It was on one of the drives called the 'beef trail', taking a herd across the northern flat lands of the Republic of Texas, that Carl first saw what he wanted; good tall grass, low tableland backed up to a low-lying mountain range. Water, he discovered, was plentiful, with a river a few miles along and signs of seasonal creeks almost everywhere.

He first saw the place when left behind with Jesus de Valdez, one of the many Mexican *vaqueros* on the ranch and a jag of cattle too sickly to keep up with the herd.

'Let them to rest up a couple days,' ordered the trail boss, 'and if they get better, walk them on. Otherwise leave them be and come on your own selves.'

Those couple days gave Carl time to ride out and look over the country. The *vaquero* didn't mind, being comfortable sitting on his blankets, using his saddle for a head rest.

'Ah, you go ahead, *compadre*,' he said smiling, 'I'll watch over these darlings and keep the coffee hot.'

It made little difference to the half-dozen head, they simply went on chomping the tall grass, never missing the rest of the herd.

For some time Carl had been thinking about finding a place and starting his own spread. It was one of the most popular subjects talked about around the campfire by nearly all the hands. Most of them were young — well, the Americans were anyway. The vaqueros on the other hand were anywhere from ten to fifteen years older. Unlike their gringo workmates, the Mexican cowboys wanted nothing more than to make enough Yankee dollars to support wives and kids.

It was Jesus' wife, Mirella, who was taking care of Rose Marie.

Once the drive was finished and the men paid off, Carl handed in his time.

'What?' exclaimed Georges Collinsworth when Carl told him he was leaving. 'What're ya gonna do? Don't forget you got yourself a young'un to look after.'

'Yep, that's why I'm moving on. Gonna go into competition with ya,' laughed Carl, pocketing the coins. 'Found myself some likely-looking grasslands up in the territories. I figure to start out with a few head we had to leave behind on the drive. Not much for making the walk to the railhead but will breed up to start my herd.'

The rancher nodded. 'Wal, if anyone can do her, it'd be you. All right, you go get yourself to building a ranch. We'll come by in a few years, I'll have the men pick up what you've got extra and run them with mine. Pay you what I get for every head when they're tallied at the railhead.'

Using the money he had saved, he hired a couple men to help him cut and limb a bunch of pine trees. He looked the land over and finally settled on one particular piece. Dragging the logs out of the high country, he started building his house. Filed his claim over the mountains at Fort Rawlins and just like that, he was his own man on his own ranch. A year or so after leaving Collinsworth he got word Jesus had been thrown by a horse and died. Riding over, he proposed to Mirella. She, being a strong Catholic said no, she was already married. But she would join him as his housekeeper. By the time Rose Marie was turning into being the beauty of the area and had cowboys lining up to hire on, his spread was showing a profit.

16

'Now then, gents,' said Jacobson, smiling and motioning his guests to the coffee, 'help yourselves and let's talk. Oh, first off, I gotta say, I heard all about you from my daughter. She was madder than hell over what she called a couple saddle tramps getting in her way in town.' His smile got even bigger. 'Raised her myself. Her ma died right after she was born. Got to admit I might have done a better job of it. Darn girl is headstrong and stubborn. Makes it hard to live with at times. But I reckon you're not out here to talk about Missy, are you?'

'No, me'n Louie here are trying to get a handle on the vigilantes. Don't really have a place to start doing what we've been hired to do. We figure you, having put up some of the money, might have some idea about things.'

'Oh,' laughed the cattleman, 'I do. Yes, I do. But you have to remember, I might have added to the pot, but I'm in a position I don't see how I can lose. You boys bring an end to the Vigilance Committee and we'll all feel a bit better. However, on the other hand, while they are catching rustlers my stock might be a bit safer and the statehood people get a black mark against them.'

Louie frowned at that. 'I'm not exactly sure how that works.'

'Well, it's simple. The Frying Pan is on 160 acres I filed on with the territorial government. That's what is legal. Now you have to look at the area. It's a big bowl with a mountain range running from the south, or south west, curving up and around. Here's my spread at the southern end. There's mountains, not real big but enough to make a good boundary in that direction,' he flipped a hand that way. 'The high country goes along acting like a barrier until it drops down at the little river, which is the end of my range. Actually, except for my 160 acres, all the land within that part of the bowl is open, public range. The way it is, though, I'm the only one can use it. So, keeping things the way they are is in my best interest.'

Louie shook his head. 'What could change? The mountains won't move and you said you've filed on this land. What could cause you trouble?'

'It's the open range. If the territory were to become a state as some people want, it'd open up the public lands for homesteading. Since the end of the war, back east, the federal government has wanted to let homesteaders move west. Seems there are a lot of men who were fighting in that war that now want their own land. Right now it's the fear of the vigilantes that is keeping the politicians back in Washington from approving statehood.'

'So on one hand,' said Buck quietly, 'they are protecting your livestock and your use of the open range by hanging rustlers. Sounds good, except I under-stand not all of the men hung are proven cattle thieves.'

'Yes,' said Jacobson, letting his almost permanent smile fade, 'that is, I'm afraid, likely. Hell, I don't think I've lost many head over the years. Not enough to worry about anyway. Oh, yeah, once in a while one or another of the folks living on smaller spreads, too small to make a good living, get hungry and they'll take a beef. But people's got to eat. No, I don't recall any of my hands telling about cattle being missing.'

'Your hands,' Buck said, glancing at Louie, 'they're not all that welcoming. That one fella, Smokey someone called him, was looking like he didn't like us much.'

Jacobson's smile was back. 'I reckon. That boy is trouble looking for a place to happen. He was coming on to being a good hand when he found he had a knack for shooting that pistol of his. Got him to thinking he was a natural born gunfighter. Some day, he's gonna brace the wrong man and . . . wal, we'll see. Now the rest of them?' he chuckled. 'Yeah, those men understand how it is for the ranch. They'll just be protecting the Frying Pan. Don't pay them no mind.'

'Our question is about the Committee. Do you have any idea who makes up that gang?'

'No sir, I don't. It isn't any of my hands and I doubt if any work for Runkle, the next rancher over. He's about in the same situation I am. Most of his range is open and would be broken up by homesteaders' fences. We've got the biggest spreads in this part of the territory and hire the most men. Oh, Fitzwalter, on over beyond Runkle's Double Bar R has a couple men working for him, but it's not hardly likely they're part of any vigilante bunch.'

It was apparent the owner of the Frying Pan wasn't going to be able to help them. Riding away from the ranch, Louie had to say, 'Don't seem that helped us much. A good cup of coffee but not much information.'

'Maybe. But I've been thinking about where a gang of men making up a vigilante committee could be. Not likely they'd be camped out in the mountains somewhere. Or come into this area just to do their dirty work. Nothing says they'd have to all come from one ranch or another either. Nope, it could be a few men from here, a few from there and even a few from town. You're right. Good coffee but we're still without a starting point.'

Louie rode quiet for a bit then laughed, 'At least no one took a shot at us. I was kinda worried about that guy with the tied-down gun. What'd they call him? Smokey?'

17

Following directions given by the cattleman, the pair crossed the river at a shallows and rode on to find the rutted stage road again. Slowly the layout of the land changed from being almost flat grassland to rolling prairie. Riding at a ground-eating trot they passed through a scattering of stunted trees, most not more than tall bushes. Coming out into the open country they noticed how the landscape changed again. Ahead and off to one side, a jagged upthrust of rock towered over the road.

Glancing at the rock face, Buck instinctively considered it a good place for an ambush. The thought barely faded when his horse shied to one side a step and a bee buzzed by his ear. The sound of a gunshot came almost instantly.

Both men reacted, reining around

115

and spurring away at a gallop. Pulling up a short distance away they sat their saddles and looked back.

'Now, dammit, Louie. Everything was going good until you said something about us getting shot at.'

'Wonder if it was the Vigilance Committee making themselves known?'

'Not likely. I reckon any vigilantes would be wanting to hang us up not shoot us. What say we take a ride over that way, see what we can see?'

With their long guns ready the two rode back toward the rocky file at a good clip. Since serving as a ranger Buck had carried three weapons, two .44 Colt Dragoons, one holstered at his side and the other in a saddle bag, and a Winchester of the same caliber as a saddle gun. Louie's rifle was a lever-action Henry. His belt gun was a cartridge-converted Colt Walker, holstered in a Slim Jim holster. More likely called a California Slim Jim, the leather holster covered most all of his revolver.

Both men kept their focus on the

rocky outcropping as they rode close. Circling around they quickly found where the shooter had tied his mount. A pile of smoking horse apples were all that was left.

'Gonna be hard to identify the horse from those,' said Louie, his eyes searching the rocks above where they had stopped.

Buck swung down and ground-hitched the stud horse. 'I'd say our friend is long gone. But keep an eye out and I'll take a look.'

Others had used this pile of rock before, leaving a faint trail winding up around boulders, some as big as houses. At the highest point, a small opening was well-guarded by more weather-rounded boulders. From there the roadway below was visible for a long stretch. It didn't take long for the big man to see the ambusher had left nothing behind.

'Nothing,' he said climbing back in saddle. 'A very likely place covering the trail, though. It's a wonder he wasn't able to make the shot.'

'Your horse side-stepped a bit,' said Louie. 'I thought you'd probably seen something, but maybe the horse did.'

'Hmm, well, whichever. It appears someone was waiting. Makes me wonder who knew we'd be coming this way.'

'Didn't make it any secret, our idea of talking to Jacobson and the other one, Runkle, did we?'

'No. But from town only the sheriff knew we were riding out this way today. Of course there were all those hands at the Frying Pan.'

'Uh huh,' said Louie slowly, 'but let's not forget our friend, Isaac Black. As I recall he's working where we're headed.'

'Oh, I haven't forgotten him. Not for a moment.'

18

The Double Bar R wasn't as well laid out or maintained as Jacobson's place was. It was obvious the main house, the pair of large hay barns and all the outbuildings hadn't seen a coat of paint in a long time. A half dozen or so head of riding stock came to the corral fence to watch the riders ride by. Buck noticed one of the horses was sweaty, foam dripping from its mouth.

Ready to greet the two were four men, standing at the rails on the porch of the main ranch house. Buck and Louie reined in and sat their saddles while taking their time to look the men over.

'What the hell y'all want here?' called down one man. Buck figured that had to be the owner, Runkle.

Standing as tall as he could, Runkle was shorter than any of the others. A banty rooster of a man, Buck thought, born small but making up for it by being pushy, louder and usually meaner. He'd run into the kind before.

From the saddles, the men were all looking eye-to-eye with the welcoming committee.

Ignoring the owner, Buck let his gaze settle on the man at one side. Standing facing Buck squarely, Black's right hand sat loosely on the butt of his cross-draw holstered six-gun. The gunman wasn't smiling.

'Well, Isaac,' said Buck easily, 'I see you didn't take time to rub your horse down after running him like that. Not the sign of a good horseman. Not that I'd ever figure you for being anything but a blow-hard would-be gunnie anyway.'

Black's face blanched. Quickly glancing around he stammered. 'I don't know what you're talking about, Ranger. Boss,' he said turning to Runkle, 'this here is the mighty Buck Armstrong. And his shadow, Louie

Lewis. A couple has-been Texas Rangers, ya know.'

'I'll ask ya again,' demanded Runkle, hands on hips, glaring at the mounted men, 'what the hell are ya after here? You're not welcome and best be turning around and riding out while ya can.'

Louie shrugged his shoulders and smiled. Buck took his time, studying each man as if he wanted to remember them. Lifting his gaze he slowly let his eyes take in the front of the house.

'Well,' he said finally, not hurrying, 'If you're counting on that damn fool Black there, I'd say we have little to worry about. Now you can stand up there and bluff and bluster all you want. But in your heart of hearts you and those standing with you know, if anyone gets pushy, you'll be the first I'll shoot.'

For a long moment nobody moved. Then, glancing first to one side then the other, Runkle nodded.

'All right. You can climb down. Won't let it be said anyone coming to the

Double Bar R ain't treated right. Boys,' he said to the others, 'I reckon y'all got something to do?'

19

Handley Runkle was a bully. There were no two ways about it. From his earliest days he had had to fight for what he got. The runt of the family, one of six boys and two girls making it past childhood, he'd always got only what the others left. Until he stole his first pistol.

Breaking a rear window of one of the general stores in New Orleans, he slid open the window and walked to the front as if it was open and he was a customer. Runkle had been given the job by the gang he was running with because of his size.

'Yeah, y'all go ahead and do it like I said,' ordered the leader of the gang, a kid named Cassidy, 'then come up and open the front door. We'll clean the place out and you'll get your share.'

It worked out about like Cassidy had

planned. He was the gang boss only because he was bigger, tougher and meaner than any of the others. The gang, made up of boys aged 12 to 18 or so, had been causing trouble since early spring. Living on the busy city streets, the gang existed by what they could steal.

It wasn't the first time Runkle had done what Cassidy ordered. This time was no different except when walking through the darkened store, Runkle spotted the glass-fronted gun case. Stopping just long enough to grab a revolver he finished his job, opening the front door. A few days later, after Cassidy had sold the goods the gang had walked out with, Runkle took his share and returned to the store where he bought a box of .38 caliber shells.

After selling the youngster the bullets, the shopkeeper thought about it a bit. What would a young kid like that want with .38 caliber bullets? Did he have anything to do with the break-in where a .38 caliber Smith & Wesson pistol had been stolen? Watching Runkle walk away he decided to talk to the town marshal. When that lawman called out to the young man, Runkle didn't hesitate. Grabbing the reins of the first horse he came to, he swung into the saddle and kicking the surprised animal in the ribs, galloped out of town.

That was his first brush with the law. But not the only one. Arrested a few years later following a botched bank robbery, Runkle was sentenced to two years in a work gang. It was his size that got him caught. A witness had noted one of the robbers had been a boy. Walking down the street the next day, the witness identified Runkle.

'I thought it was a boy,' the witness explained to the marshal, 'but the way he walked, swaggering down the street like he owned it. Yes, sir. He's one of them.'

Being small, the deputy overseeing the work gang put Runkle to work carrying a water pail from a nearby creek to the prisoners. It didn't take Runkle long to realize the deputy couldn't very well leave the work gang. On the next trip to the creek, Runkle tossed the bucket into the brush and kept going.

He figured he was about twenty-five the next time he stood before a judge. It was in Las Vegas, New Mexico and the charge was beating up a girl in one of the town's better brothels. The girl stood tall in her high-necked bright red linen dress and told the judge, 'Yes, your Honour. It was that little bastard right there what left me all bruised up. He just turned crazy when I told him I didn't do what he wanted me to do. So he hit me. Not once but two or three times. Here,' she said, starting to unbutton the front of her dress, 'I'll show you the bruises.'

20

The judge quickly stopped her, saying he believed what she was saying. Runkle was sentenced to two years in the county jail. It was there Runkle met Henry Morse. A bounty hunter had brought Morse in claiming the reward put out for his arrest. The town marshal locked Morse up and sent a telegram to the person offering the reward. Runkle and Morse had nearly a week, sitting in a cell and talking before Morse was released. The response the marshal had received said the reward was no longer offered.

With nothing to do, Runkle sat on the hard wood bench and counted the days. It was Morse who came to his rescue. By offering the prisoner a job, the judge had agreed to free Runkle as long as he promised not to go anywhere near the brothel or the women he'd beaten up.

It was an easy promise to make. The job Morse had for Runkle was in the saloon and brothel he owned. Runkle stayed with Morse for a year or two before moving on. It was about five years later the two got together again. In that time Morse had sold his saloon and gone out to California. Meanwhile Runkle headed the other way, back to New Orleans. There he fell into partnership with a woman almost as tough as he was. The saloon they operated was owned by a wealthy shipping family who made their fortune bringing rum from the Caribbean. That partnership lasted until Runkle was caught stealing from the till. When he left town, again on a stolen horse, he took along the son he'd fathered with his partner. The woman, glad to get rid of both the boy and his father, didn't make a big thing of it.

The man whose horse Runkle had stolen had, on the other hand, sworn out a warrant for his arrest.

21

Isaac Black was the last of the hands to walk off, leaving Runkle standing alone on the porch. Buck could almost feel the heavy threat in the gunman's eyes.

'C'mon up,' said the little boss man finally, motioning to Buck and Louie. 'We can sit while we talk.'

Up close it was easy to see the man's thin face, his beady eyes dark and part hidden under thick eye-brows. Runkle hadn't aged well; coarse wrinkles fanned from the corner of his eyes lining his sunken cheeks. Taking one of the bare wooden chairs he sat down and after motioning the two to other chairs, sat and glared.

'Don't bother asking me anything about the vigilantes. I ain't bothered by them or by any two-bit rustling.'

Buck nodded. 'But still you helped with the pot we're going to be paid with. How'd that happen?'

'Ah, hell. It don't mean nothing. Like giving a beef to that preacher there in town so he could help feed some broken-down sod buster. Don't mean nothing. I gotta live in this country, don't I? Wal, sometimes that means making nice. Don't think I really care, though. Cuz I don't. All right, so there's some idiots going around hanging other fools who think they can take what don't belong to them. I ain't seen none of my livestock going missing. Not so's you'd know, anyhow.'

'Uh huh. From what we've been told, you'd most likely let the vigilantes go on hanging men, whether actual rustlers or not, to keep holding off any move toward statehood. Is that your thinking?'

Before responding Runkle shifted his gaze toward Louie. 'He don't say much, does he? Hey, boy, you a Mexican? I was down there in Texas when we fought your people. Took Texas and by golly most of this territory away from the bean-eaters. Yes, by damn if we didn't. I ain't had no Mexican on the place since then.'

'Sí, señor,' responded Louie in a heavy, lazy accent, 'I am for sure a part Mexicano. A big part. You don't like my kind, that's your problem. Fact is, I don't much like you or your kind either. Not that I'm ever going to let people like you bother me. Y'all carry around so much hate you don't have room to breathe easy. Likely don't get much time to enjoy life either. But again that's your problem, not mine. No, I don't talk much. Don't have anything to say to you.'

For a long moment Runkle sat glaring at Louie before turning away. 'All right. You've said your piece. And yes,' he looked at Buck, 'you got it. The damn fools wanting to make this a state. All they think about is themselves. A state. Just gives more idiots the right to tell us how to live. Bah. Who in hell cares if it's a state or a territory?'

Buck chuckled. 'Might say you're

pretty strong on it, huh?'

'Don't mean nothing. Don't mean I got anything to do with no hanging foolishness neither. So what'd you come all the way out here for?'

'Just getting an idea of what it's all about. Have to start somewhere and meeting the men who're involved is as good a place as any.'

'Wal, now you've met me. And didn't learn nothing. Yeah, I put some money in the pot. That way I win no matter what. The fool vigilantes get stopped or not — don't matter to me. Unless y'all do stop them then I could end up losing out use of the open range. Damn foolishness. That land ain't no good for nothing but cattle. Damn farmer come in and ruin it, they would. Government don't care. That's when me and others like me would lose out. Damn foolishness, I say.'

Buck nodded and stood up. 'Yes, I got that. Can't say you're alone with that feeling, but there it is. We'll do what we can, what we were hired to do.'

Turning, he started off the porch but stopped. 'One other thing. You've got a boy. We met him in town a day or so back. He was with your gunhand, Isaac Black. Just to let you know, I'll likely have to shoot Black before it's all over. Might be a good idea to keep your son away from him.'

Runkle came out of the chair, suddenly all red-faced. 'Don't you be telling me anything about my boy. And don't be thinking I give a hoot if'n you and that damn gunnie Black go to pulling iron against each other. Now I'll give ya a warning; Black's fast. Wouldn't be surprised if'n he dropped ya. And likely your Mexican sidekick, too.'

Buck glanced at Louie and smiled. 'All right,' he said turning back to Runkle, 'you've had your say. Just don't let your boy get in the way, is all I'm saying. We'll bid you a good day.' Touching the brim of his hat, he went down and got into the saddle.

Again side by side, they rode out of

the yard. 'He's a mighty angry man,' said Louie, his head turning side to side, watching. 'Now all we got to do is ride away from this spread without getting shot.'

22

Back on the main road the two men rode warily, keeping a close watch on the surrounding landscape. Twice they had passed rutted ranch roads going off to the west; Fitzwalter's Mustang Ranch, they'd been told, was the only one to the east, toward the foothills. When they saw the log gate at the ranch road it was obvious they had found the right place. A sign announcing the ranch hung crookedly from one side of the gate. Three men sat relaxed on the log fence fronting the stage road. Another man sat his saddle off to the side.

'I reckon you've gone far enough,' called out one of the men, jumping down off the fence. 'This here's private property. The boss, he don't like any trespassers coming in.'

The riders pulled up and took their

time looking things over. Buck looked everywhere but toward the man sitting his horse. Finally, after a long moment, he glanced in that direction and smiled.

'Well, look here, Louie. I'd say that was the jasper what came in to tell us he was going to shoot us. What was his name? Uh, oh, yes, Yarberry.' Glancing to his partner, he nodded, then looked back at the man, who hadn't moved. 'As I recall, he didn't impress me much at the time. Did he you?'

From the moment they had stopped at the gate, Louie had been watching Yarberry. Not looking at Buck he simply shook his head.

'Naw. And now here he is. Hey, there, is this when you plan on earning your money?'

Yarberry snorted and reined his horse around and rode away down the ranch road, not looking back.

'I gotta hand it to ya,' said the man standing by the fence. 'There ain't too many what'd talk to that jasper like you just did. He's not one what's got a sense of humour. Wonder he didn't shoot you down where ya sat. But never mind. We've got our orders. Nobody gets by here without the bosses saying it's OK. So just turn back and ride out.'

While Buck had been talking to Yarberry the other two men had climbed down and, with thumbs hooked in their gunbelts, hands close to their revolver grips, spread out to each side.

'You men are certainly not very welcoming,' said Buck, slouching in the saddle. 'Louie, I guess we'd better not bother these gentlemen. Boys, we can tell we're not wanted. You tell your boss-man, Mr Fitzwalter, we was here and would like to talk to him about the vigilante problem. Would hate to think that's why he's so shy.'

Reining the big black around, Buck rode back to the stage road. Louie sat for a minute watching the three men, then nodding, followed.

'Well, partner,' Buck said glancing back over his shoulder at the men who had regained their place on the fence, 'that strike you as being interesting?'

'A little,' said Louie, taking the makings out of his shirt pocket and rolling a cigarette. 'Seems a waste of three cow hands, having them ride a fence like that. Wonder what's going on they don't want anyone to see.'

'Uh huh. Not likely any vigilantes. That breed of men work better when nobody's around to see what they do. Nope. Does make me wonder, though.'

'One thing's clear. We now know who's paying that Yarberry fellow. You ever have a run-in with this Fitzwalter?'

'Not that I remember. The name isn't familiar. Maybe he just doesn't like anyone who rode with the Rangers.'

23

It was coming on dark by the time the two men got back to Auburn. Supper time. The next morning, after they enjoyed a big breakfast, they found a couple spindle-backed chairs on the hotel porch.

'Well, Buck, tell me if I'm wrong, but that ride out to those ranches yesterday didn't do us much good, did it?'

'No, not much. But there isn't really anything else we can do, except keep talking to people. Sooner or later someone'll tell us something that will give us a direction to that so-called Vigilance Committee, or,' he paused before going on, 'or sooner or later those on the Committee will come calling.'

'That supposed to make me feel good? Let's hope it's sooner rather than later. There's already been one hanging since we took on this job. That didn't help us either. I'm hoping there aren't any more.'

'Hey, look who's coming our way. Good morning, Sheriff,' Buck called out as two men came up on the porch.

'Buck, Louie, want you to meet Marshal Calhoun. From over at Fort Rawlins. Marcus, these are the two men I was telling you about.'

'Good morning, gents. Angus tells me you were both Texas Rangers and now you're here to stop the vigilantes.'

Buck chuckled. 'Angus. Now that's the first I've heard you even had a front name, Sheriff. Yeah,' he turned back to the marshal, 'and we were told you don't get over this way very often. What's the occasion?'

'Now that's not exactly true. Riding the stage over here isn't the most pleasant way to spend the best part of the day, but I come over every time I need to. Angus tells me you spent most of yesterday out talking to some of the ranchers. That right?'

Buck nodded. 'Not that we learned much. But yes, we did get to sit down with a couple of the bigger ranch owners.'

'See anyone that somehow didn't fit in?'

'Don't know what you mean, exactly. Most everyone we met would be doing about what you'd expect. Oh,' he hesitated, 'with the exception of Harry Yarberry. Run into him at one place. Haven't figured out what he's doing, though.'

'Who's this Yarberry?' asked the sheriff.

'A gunfighter,' Marshal Calhoun answered. 'Got himself quite a reputation for hiring his gun out to just about anybody. You say you ran into him. And there was no gunplay?'

Louie chuckled. 'Nope. He's made it clear, though, what his intentions are. Says he's going to shoot both of us.'

'It just wasn't the right time or place,' said Buck. 'Those kind like things going their way before they pull iron on someone. Our meeting up with him yesterday wasn't in his favour. He didn't have the advantage.'

'Where was this meeting?'

'At the Mustang Ranch. We wanted to talk with the owner, a man named Fitzwalter.'

Marshal Calhoun nodded. 'Fitzwalter, huh. There's been some rumours floating around about a Fitzwalter and his ranch. Haven't been able to prove anything, but from what I've been hearing, this ranch is a good place to spend some time if you want to stay out of sight for a while. That's why I came over to Auburn. There's a fellow, Hyman Neil, was seen over in town. A real bad man. From over in New Mexico. The Federal Marshal over there telegraphed around for everyone to be on the lookout for him. Appears folk over that way really want to get their hands on him.'

'And you think he might be coming this way?' asked the sheriff.

'Well, from what the marshal said, both Neil and Fitzwalter were friendly back when Fitzwalter ran a saloon over there. I used that as an excuse to come over to Auburn.'

'And I thought you just wanted me to take you fishing.'

'That too. But this is serious. The marshal says Neil is the baddest cowboy of them all.'

24

There wasn't much happening in Auburn after the two lawmen went back toward the sheriff's office. Marshal Calhoun didn't have any more to say about the outlaw, Neil.

'I wonder,' said Louie as the two walked back down the street, 'if the good sheriff is actually going to take the marshal fishing.'

Sitting back with his boot heels hooked under the porch railing, Buck smiled. 'I got the idea Sheriff McDonald only goes down to the river with his fishing pole when he thinks something is going to happen that'd be too big for him to handle.'

For a time neither man said anything. Watching a wagon come in held their interest for a while. Nothing was said but both were sure the man and woman sitting high on the wagon seat were coming from one of the smaller ranches. They somehow didn't have the look of being too prosperous. As the wagon passed by the man nodded to the two sitting on the porch. Two children poked their heads from under a canvas tarp stretched over the wagon bed. A boy and a girl. The girl gave Buck and Louie a little wave with her smile. The boy, slightly older, simply stared.

That bit of excitement was barely over when Mayor Winterbottom came out of his store. Standing on the plank sidewalk, he watched as the wagon stopped. Stepping down off the sidewalk he helped the woman climb down. As the couple went up and into the store, Winterbottom glanced over to the two men sitting on the hotel porch. Nodding to them, he turned and followed his customers.

Louie took a long look up at the sky. 'Hey, Buck. What's today? Isn't Saturday by any chance is it?'

'Don't think so. Maybe those folks

ran out of coffee and had to come in early. Life gets hard when you don't have your coffee.'

'Ah, I won't argue with ya on that. Tell you what, I'll flip a coin to see who goes across and brings us back a cup. What do ya say?'

Buck smiled and reached into his pants pocket. Flipping the coin high in the air he caught it and slapped it down on the back of his hand as Louie called out 'Heads.'

'Well,' Buck smiled, 'it's tails.' He put the coin back in his pocket. 'I'll have mine black, if you don't mind.'

'Knew I should've used my own coin,' said Louie disgustedly as he got up and walked away.

Sipping their coffee they watched as a few men rode slowly in, tying up at the hitchrail in front of the saloon.

'Seems pretty early for that, don't you think?' Louie remarked.

'Yep, this coffee does the job pretty fine, though. Thank you.'

Louie snorted.

146

Soon the ranching family came out of the store with the mayor following along, carrying a box of groceries. As the wagon turned and headed back the way it'd come, Winterbottom watched. Looking back at the store, he shrugged and came over to the hotel porch.

'Morning gentlemen. You two keeping an eye on things, are you?'

'Yeah,' said Louie, 'not much happening though. Guess that's about right, a town this size.'

'Uh huh. Gets busier come Saturday. Say, you haven't seen my daughter come riding in, have you?'

Buck shook his head. 'Gone for a morning ride has she?'

'No, damn it. Went out about dark last evening and didn't come in. Either of you got family?'

Both men shook their heads.

'Well, maybe that's good.'

Buck nodded. 'Likely your daughter rode out to see her friend, Rose Marie, and stayed the night. Probably nothing to worry about.'

'I want to think that, but lately she's been acting strange. Ah, hell, this isn't the first night she's stayed out. I don't know what to think.'

Nether of the two men could think of anything to say. After a moment Winterbottom sighed and stepped off the porch. 'Guess it don't do any good, standing here worrying about it. Better get back to the store.' With a little wave he walked away.

Buck watched the man thinking how maybe he was lucky not to have anyone to cause him to worry. Louie glanced the other way, watching a small bunch of horsemen come riding in.

'That looks a lot like our friend Black, doesn't it?' he asked quietly.

One of the horses was reined over toward the hotel while the others rode on down the street. Stopping at the hotel hitchrail, a man stepped off the animal, looped the reins over the bar and stepped up on the porch. The others, Buck noticed, stopped down at the saloon.

'Morning, gents,' the man said, taking off his hat and idly wiping the inner band, 'I'm Henry Raymond Fitzwalter. Understand you came by my spread, the Mustang Ranch, yesterday. I apologize for my men stopping you at the gate. They thought it best. Too many times we've had strangers come wandering in. I've got too many livestock running free not to be cautious. Mind if I join you a bit? We can talk things over.'

Buck nodded, and the man pulled over another chair. Fitzwalter wasn't your usual horse wrangler. Wearing low-heeled, high-topped shoes made that clear. Instead of canvas pants, or even denim like nearly every other rider wore, he had on black wool pants and three-button suit coat. The kind usually seen in the big cities, worn mostly by bankers and lawyers. Sitting down, Fitzwalter slipped the buttons on his suit coat, flipping both sides open as if to get air moving around his chest. Both Buck and Louie saw the shoulder holster hanging under his left armpit. The silver gun butt of his pistol sparkled in the morning sunshine.

'I gather you're the team hired by the town to see about getting rid of those calling themselves the Vigilance Committee. Having any luck?'

Buck shook his head. 'Not so you'd notice. That's what we was doing yesterday, riding around talking to the ranchers, trying to get a starting place with things.'

'Ah, well, yes. I'd guess it'd be hard to find that gang. They don't seem to hang around long after doing their work.'

'That's true. Fact is, there was a man left hanging from the bridge just the other day. Some youngster coming into town spotted him. Only sign of who'd put him at the end of a rope was the paper pinned to his shirt. Those on the Committee seem to think highly of themselves.'

'From the bridge, you say. They've used that bridge before once or twice. I don't envy you the job. Hard to see how you're going to catch them.'

'Yeah. Unless they do something stupid, which we're counting on.'

'Well, I don't see how I can help you any. I suppose others have told you how most of us ranchers feel about it. Would be good to get rid of this Committee but at the same time they're doing us a favour, protecting our livestock.'

Louie was keeping an eye on the saloon and noticed when Black came out to stand on the boardwalk, thumbs hooked in his belt, staring down the street at the hotel porch. After a few minutes he turned back into the bar.

'You got a hired hand there,' Louie said, 'Isaac Black. He's by way of being an old friend of ours.'

'Ike? Well, yes, he's been on my payroll for a couple months. Not all my hands are kept busy saddle-breaking our rough stock. Someone like Ike is useful in keeping my livestock from getting stolen. Those vigilantes have just about made him unnecessary, but, well,

I'd rather take care of things myself. With hands like Ike Black.'

Nothing else was said and after a few minutes Fitzwalter stood up and, nodding at the two men, walked his horse down to the saloon.

'Not many cowboys would bother walking that far,' said Louie, 'not when they could ride.'

Buck nodded, 'and not many ranchers would have someone like Isaac Black on their payroll. Wonder what all he does to earn his pay.'

25

Two events, unconnected in any way, had brought Henry Raymond Fitzwalter to financial success. A very comfortable and secure kind of success. At least it would be for a while.

Fitzwalter didn't start out life with that name; it was one he'd picked up when the name he'd been born with got too much notice. Notice of the wrong people. No, back when he was a youngster, he had been known as Henry Morse.

For the next few years after walking away from his pa's farm he worked in many places, mostly saloons and whorehouses. Being a man not afraid to use a short iron bar, his favourite weapon, his reputation as a bouncer grew. In time it was his own saloons and brothels he was protecting. The iron bar was replaced by a six-shot Smith & Wesson .38 caliber pistol which he wore in his left armpit in a leather shoulder holster.

Operating a brothel or saloon he got to meet everyone; politicians, outlaws and just your common man. Meet them and learn about them. He learned how to dress like them, leaving behind the rough working clothes of your everyday saddle tramp. Watching and learning he discovered most didn't last very long in their business. Politicians got voted out when people got angry, outlaws got shot or caught and hung, and too often businessmen got too greedy. On the other hand the common man rarely made much money.

He was thinking those deep and dark thoughts one morning when Harry Yarberry came to his saloon.

'Harry, old son, what are you doing out in the sunshine this early in the day?'

'Don't be yammering at me, Henry. I

got troubles enough without you bitching at me.'

'What's the trouble, Harry?'

'They's a fellow come into town last night. He's been asking questions. I think he's a bounty hunter.'

'Bounty hunter? Looking for you? Who put a bounty on ya?'

'It's one from a while back. Down in Jack County. Some woman claimed I shot her husband. Don't know if the money on it is still good, but I don't need some idiot coming around asking too many questions.'

'No, Harry, I can see that. Any way I can help you out?'

'You got some idea where I can hide out for a while? Long enough for things to die down? I'd pay good money for such a place.'

Henry shook his head. 'No, afraid not.'

Harry's problem stuck with him long after the killer had left. The solution to the problem came with the second event in Henry's life.

26

Henry took the stage road from Fort Rawlins toward Auburn, aiming to visit an old friend of his, Handley Runkle. The two had once been partners in a saloon and brothel down in New Mexico. Runkle now owned a cattle ranch while he was still in the saloon business. Wanting to become more than a saloon keeper, he invited himself to the Double Bar R ranch.

'Well, Henry,' explained Runkle when the two men got together, 'right now running this kind of spread is pretty good. Out there's a thousand acres or more of open range. But it ain't gonna last. A few years and this territory becomes a state and that'll be the end of it. With statehood will come homesteaders and that's the end of the open range. Fences'll spring up and trying to raise a likely herd will get tougher.'

'Didn't you say you've got near a thousand acres filed on?'

'Well, closer to about half that. But I might not be able to keep it all. When I filed on the 160 acres I was allowed I had some men working for me to file on their own 160. Then I bought them out. Gave each of them fifty dollars and they signed their homesteads over. Gives me rights to enough range and the way it's laid out, control of a lot more open range.

'This valley is huge, Henry. Old Jacobson's got most of the south-half covered. Across the river that's in-between us on south he's got at least as much open range as I got. Mine runs all the way up toward those foothills there. An old man, name of Price, has got himself a horse ranch up there. Right up against those mountains. Raises riding stock he sells to us ranchers.'

'That range of mountains, isn't Fort Rawlins just there on the other side?'

Runkle nodded. 'Yeah, about twenty

miles, I'd guess. But it's pretty hard travelling in places. Not many people bother. They usually come like you did, around the end of that stretch of foothills. The stage road stays pretty much on the flatlands that way. Might take a while longer but it's by far a lot easier.'

'But hard or not, there is a trail over those mountains?'

'Yeah, I reckon. Not good enough to run cattle over so it don't get used much. Why you asking?'

'Well,' said Henry pensively, 'say you had that spread there, right up against the mountains, and nobody else close by to see what you was doing. And there's that mostly unused trail over from Fort Rawlins. From over there you've got the whole of northern Texas and New Mexico out there in front of you. Now say you was looking for a quick way to get away from over there. I know of a number of people who'd pay big money for a place to hide out. Say a place that was safe and a long way from anyone looking for them. A place they could rest while any of those hunting them had time to move on. Now that spread would be a money-maker, wouldn't it?'

'Sounds good. But old man Price, doubt he'd be willing to sell.'

'Oh, he could be dealt with. I'm sure there's away around that.'

27

'Seems like we sit here long enough,' said Buck watching Fitzwalter disappear into the saloon, 'everyone will come by sooner or later.'

Louie grunted. 'So far none of them have bothered to bring us a cup of coffee. Not too much of anything on the vigilantes, either. Do you still think we'll get around to earning our money? Money we haven't seen yet?'

'Oh, can't see why not. I've been thinking about it. Here they are, a gang of men going around hanging rustlers, or men they claim to be rustlers. From what we've been told this is something fairly new to the area, having a gang taking credit for their work. Makes me wonder why. Why now and not, say, five years ago? Thinking about the possible reasons, the best I've come up with is the impact newspaper stories are having with statehood. All right, if that's it then one or more of the people we've been talking to has close ties to the Vigilance Committee. Now if so, I reckon it won't be long before we hear from them. However, all that thinking and reasoning has made me dry. Do you want to go over to the saloon for a beer, or the restaurant for coffee?'

'Hmm. I kinda like sitting here, watching things happen in this quiet little town. Very relaxing. Anyway, it's a mite too early in the day for beer. Wouldn't want to cause that Isaac Black any grief either. How about it's your turn to go for coffee?'

Buck thought about it a moment then nodded. Picking up the empty cups he strolled away, Louie leaned his chair back against the hotel wall and smiled. It was, in his view, shaping up to be a good morning. Be time enough for beer sometime after lunch. Anyway, sitting here, no telling who'd be coming by. Right interesting, he mused, for such a little town.

He didn't have long to wait for that to happen. Buck had barely gone into the restaurant when Louie saw someone come out of the general store.

'Will you looky there,' he said to himself. 'If that isn't Miss Mathilda herself.'

He watched as the young woman came across the street.

'Mr Lewis,' she called out before coming up to the porch, 'may I speak to you a moment?'

'Well, certainly. Come on up and take a chair. Buck's gone for coffee. He'll be back in a bit.'

'There's something I'd like to talk to you about. Pa told me he'd been worried about me and how he'd mentioned it to you. I just wanted to let you know I got home all right. Oh, and I wanted to apologize for my making fun of you the other day. About Rose Marie running you down? That wasn't very nice of me and, well, I apologize.'

Louie chuckled. 'No need. Looking at it one way it must have been real comical, seeing her trying to keep her horse under control. Probably never realized how close she came to causing Buck and me some real hurt. Never mind. How is your friend, Rose Marie? Me'n Buck were out to the Frying Pan yesterday. Talked to her pa but didn't see her.'

'Oh, Rose is fine, I guess. I haven't seen her since she was in town.' She hesitated then smiled at the man. 'If you're trying to ask if that's where I spent last night, I'll tell you. It wasn't.' She laughed and turned to step off the porch. 'My father came out directly and asked me. I didn't tell him either. I'm grown up and what I do is my business. Good day.'

The coffee, when Buck got back, had cooled just enough to be drinkable. Nodding his thanks, Louie sipped and thought.

'Never guess who came by while you was gone,' he said finally. 'I reckon it was the best of those coming to talk to us so far today.'

163

'Now who'd that be? About the only person we've missed this morning is that newspaper fella. I kinda expected him to come over to find out what we found out yesterday. He's the only one I can think of.'

Louie shook his head. 'Nope. It was the mayor's daughter, Mathilda. I kinda like that name, Mathilda. Has a real womanly sound to it.'

'So, the young lady is back home after a night of being missing. Bet that makes her pa feel better.'

'Uh huh. Maybe. But him not knowing where she was probably doesn't sit well with him. I know it wouldn't me, if'n I was in his shoes.'

'Yeah. Did she mention where she'd been?'

'Nope. Came by to apologize for the way she was laughing at us. I tried to ask her where she'd been, without coming right out and asking her, you know. But she just laughed. Said she was grown up and didn't have to account to anyone.'

Buck sipped his coffee and nodded. 'Yeah, youngsters all reach that age where they think they've got all the answers.'

'I've been thinking about it,' said Louie, 'and I'll bet I know who she was with.'

'Oh? And what did you come up with?'

'Isaac Black,' he said, and waited for a reaction. Not getting one he explained. 'First off they're of an age, wouldn't you say? Black might be a couple years older but ya gotta admit he's got a way about him that a young woman might find attractive. Little Mathilda might easily be taken by him. What got me to thinking about him was her showing up at home about the same time as his coming into town. I can't see there being too many young men in the area could hold a candle to Black for a young woman who's just getting to the age of being frisky. Yup, that's the way I got it figured.'

Buck put his empty cup down and

smiled. 'Well, if that's the way of it, the mayor could have more to trouble him than a gang of vigilantes. Sure glad she isn't my child.'

28

The rest of the day went along quiet and, far as Louie was concerned, tiresome.

'Damn it, Buck, we aren't getting much done to earn our money. Sitting around all day wasn't too bad but can't we think of something better to do with our time?'

'Yeah, I kinda agree. So, tonight after supper we'll have a drink over at the saloon, then bed down. All the time I'll be thinking of something to do so you won't go on being bored. And you do the same. Tomorrow, rather than simply sitting around we'll compare what we've thought of and, by golly, we'll do it. Whatever 'it' is. Now, does that make you feel better?'

'No.'

Buck laughed.

That was about what happened, until

shortly after finishing their breakfast the next day. They were standing on the boardwalk outside the restaurant, Louie was picking the bits of crisp pan-fried ham from his teeth, when a rider rode in pulling a pack horse behind him.

'We've seen this fella before, haven't we?'

'Louie, your eyesight is good but your memory needs some work. Coming our way is the gunfighter we ran into out at the Frying Pan. Smokey, someone called him.'

'I do believe you're right. Wonder who the fella what's draped over his pack horse is.'

Stopping in front of the sheriff's office. Smokey tied both horses to the hitchrail and pushed open the office door. A few minutes later Sheriff McDonald came out and, lifting a corner of the tarp covering the body, looked. Shaking his head, he glanced across toward Buck and Louie.

'Hey, there,' he called. 'C'mon over. This might be of interest to y'all.'

Smokey stood in the doorway rolling a cigarette, smiling at Buck and Louie.

'Thought it might be what you're wanting,' he said, smirking. 'Too bad you didn't catch that gang of vigilantes before they got to this jasper, though.'

'Where'd you find him?' asked Buck after looking at the dead man's face. Louie looked then shook his head.

'Out close to our line shack, south of the home ranch. And before ya ask, no, I don't recognize him at all.'

Buck nodded. 'You found him hanging?'

'Yup. Just off to the side, in a little gully. Almost outa sight, he was. It was a bunch of crows yammering around that caught my attention. They hadn't done much damage to him so I don't figure he'd been there long. Probably late yesterday, I reckon.'

'Anything in his pockets,' asked the sheriff, 'to tell us who he is? Was?'

'Nope. And this time weren't no paper pinned to his shirt neither. But as far as we there at the ranch know, ain't been nobody out that way for a couple weeks. I cut him down and took him back to the ranch. Didn't know but what Mr Jacobson might want a look. Hell, he might have wanted to plant him up on the ridge in the ranch cemetery. The old man's got some funny ideas. But he said no. Best if I brung him into town. Let the sheriff know. Guess he's all yours now, Sheriff.'

'You're sure he was a rustler?' asked Buck.

'Oh yeah. There was what's left of a bit of a fire. Looked like a cinch ring leaning against a rock. All fire-blackened like he'd been using it to put his brand on livestock. I've seen things like that before.'

'Did you see any livestock anywhere without the Frying Pan brand?'

'Nope. We ain't been out into that corner much since earlier in the spring. Probably be another month before we make a gather out there. Could be a lot of cattle out that way. Lots of those little gullies, ya know. Runoff from the foothills cut new ones every winter. Damn cows like to get back in there and hide. Can be hard work getting them out. Let me tell ya, harder getting the yearlings out to a branding fire than I think they're worth.'

'Could you take Louie and me out to where you found him?'

'Sure could. I figure to go back anyhow. Do what I was sent out to do, check on the condition of the line shack.'

Sheriff McDonald untied the pack horse lead. 'I'll take this fella down to the undertaker's place while you get your animals saddled up.'

29

Nobody said much as the three rode out of town. Crossing the bridge they rode on, turning off a ways before the Frying Pan ranch road. The pack horse Smokey was leading no longer carrying a load; the dead man was being taken care of by the undertaker. Sheriff McDonald thought he could get the local business community to cover the cost of a pine box and burial in the town cemetery.

'Quicker to cut across here,' said Smokey. 'Unless ya want to go on to the ranch, talk to Mr Jacobson.'

Buck shook his head. 'No reason to now. Maybe later. Let's go see what we can. Whoever hung that fellow up might have left something behind.'

'I didn't seen nothing.'

For the most part the country they were riding through was flat grassland.

Way off to one side Louie spotted a half-dozen or so head of longhorns. The cattle stood watching the riders, slowly coming together in a bunch. It was a natural movement. The cattle wary of anything out of the ordinary, bunching up for protection. Smokey and the other two ignored the cattle and rode on.

'Y'all do much of this kind of work?' Smokey asked at one point. 'Looks to me like it'd be easy money. Coming into a place and cleaning out the bad guys.'

Louie chuckled. 'Might look easy but at times it's damn slow going.'

'To answer your question,' said Buck, 'no. We don't do a lot of work like this. And I'm getting the feeling we shouldn't have said OK when they asked us to come to Auburn.'

'What would ya usually be doing?'

Louie chuckled. 'We were on our way to California when a friend asked us to stop and see what we could do.'

'Y'all were Rangers, weren't ya?

Someone said ya were.'

'Yeah, we were until invited to turn in our badges.'

'Were ya rangers long? During the war with Mexico?'

'No,' answered Buck, 'I joined after that was over and Louie a little later.'

'Ever shoot someone? When ya were a Ranger, I mean.'

Buck frowned. 'Things like that happened. I wasn't ever in any kind of shoot-out like the newspapers back east like to write about. That kind of stuff is, for the most part, garbage. Can't say about Louie, though. I do know he gets a mite upset when folks ask him embarrassing questions. I'd be a little cautious, was I you.'

Smokey glanced at Louie but didn't ask any more questions.

30

The place the young cowboy led them to was a small swale off to one side of a grown-over trail. For the past hour they'd been riding single-file along the trail. Buck thought it looked like something the cattle would use getting from one water hole to another. Actually, the place Smokey pulled up to looked almost like the mouth of a small box canyon.

'Down there,' he said, pointing down off the trail. 'If they'd used a tree back a bit more I'd never have seen him.'

Buck stood in the stirrups and took a long look around. 'Not much different here than anywhere else. How far is that line cabin you were heading to, Smokey?'

'Oh, another hour's ride I reckon.'

'Hmm, Louie, it's getting late in the afternoon. What say we find a place over there for our bedrolls and settle in? Get us an early start in the morning looking the place over.' Louie nodded and started reining his horse down, stopping at the mouth of the shallow canyon.

Smokey sat for a moment then followed along. 'You don't mind, I'll join ya. Probably wouldn't make it to the cabin before it got too dark to see.'

From where the men unrolled their sleeping bags they could just see where the dead man's fire had been.

'There ain't much there,' said Smokey, 'some ashes and a burned black cinch ring. I simply unloaded the supplies was on the back of the pack horse and strung them up in another tree, safe from any varmint. Wrapped him up in a blanket and tied him to the back of my pack horse. I never did see any sign of his horse or even a saddle.'

Throwing together a quick, hot little blaze, a supper of crisp bacon, fried bread and canned peaches was eaten, washed down with coffee boiled in a large can. With supper out of the way the three sat around enjoying their smokes.

Camping out along the trail was something both Buck and Louie favoured. Lying back watching the stars, or the moon if it had risen, after a day of riding was very pleasant. Smokey glanced from one to the other, wondering if they'd mind his asking questions. Finally he had enough of the evening's quiet. 'When y'all was Texas Rangers,' he asked concentrating on rolling a cigarette, 'did ya ever capture any rustlers?' Using a stick poked into the fire, he lit his cigarette.

'No,' said Buck, using a bigger stick to poke at the fire. 'All the time I was with the Rangers, I rarely got involved with chasing down gangs of cattle rustlers. Heard a lot of stories about it though. Seems there was a lot of trouble with Mexican rustlers along the border just after the end of the Civil War. The Mexs would come into the

Republic of Texas, this was before Texas became a state, and run herds across the river. Of course there were also reports of Americans going south and coming back with herds of Mexican cattle. Listening to the stories I got the idea it was tough keeping a herd anywhere close to either side of the border.'

'Hmm, yeah,' commented Louie after a moment. 'I was part of a detachment sent out in the Fort Griffin area to see what could be done about a vigilante gang who had been working to put down an epidemic of horse thieving. We did a lot of riding and about the only thing we saw was a man hanging from a pecan tree. Funny thing was leaning up against the tree trunk was a well-worn pick and shovel. We reckoned the tools were in case someone wanted to dig a grave.'

31

'I've heard it said,' said Smokey, 'getting caught stealing a horse was a sure-fire way to get hung while slapping a brand on someone's unbranded calf could be overlooked.'

'Wal, yeah. That could happen,' said Louie nodding. 'Taking a man's horse might be leaving him stranded in dangerous country. Or out there where the nearest water was miles away. Lots of cattlemen work on the assumption of a failure to brand a new calf meant the critter could be lost real quick.'

Nothing was said for a while. The three men relaxed, staring into the fire, probably thinking about the man who'd been hung in the tree they were camped near.

'Wasn't always only men who did the rustling. Don't think it was,' said Buck after a bit.

Smokey came alert, frowning. 'Women rustlers? I never heard such a thing.'

'Oh yeah. It happened. One story I heard had to do with a woman named Kate Averell. She was about sixteen when she married a fella named Pickell. He was a few years older and not a good man. It was said he abused her, going so far as to use a whip on her. That was somewhere in Kansas. A few years later Kate turned up in Red Cloud, Nebraska without her husband. Don't know what happened to him. She worked as a cook in an establishment thought to be a brothel. Whether she was a prostitute or not I don't know. But it wasn't long before she married again, a fella named Jim Henderson. The couple moved down to the Texas Panhandle and each filed on 160 acres. To start their ranch Kate was said to have bought a couple dozen head from a fella passing through. Soon, a rider travelling through the area said he counted more'n fifty head on the couple's 320-acre spread. Well, according to the story, Kate filed a brand and when anyone asked about how fast her herd was growing she explained she'd been gathering mavericks. You know, unbranded cattle. It wasn't long before people were calling her 'Cattle Queen Kate'.

'Well, there was a big cattleman, name of Bothwell, who had his operation a couple miles down the road. It was said this Bothwell had gotten tired of Kate putting her brand on his young stuff. It was a lot like here, everybody was running their stock on their own homesteaded land as well as open range. A range detective, George Rawlins, went to work for Bothwell and after a while accused Kate of rustling cattle from Bothwell and branding them with her brand.

'Bothwell and a few of his hands rode over and arrested Kate and her husband. One of Kate's hired hands, Dan Fitger, tried to stop them and a gun battle started up. It ended pretty quick when Kate's man was run off, leaving one of Bothwell's hands wounded. Fitger rode over to another ranch but by the time he got back, both Kate and Jim had been hung. Bothwell was arrested by Rangers but there hadn't been any witnesses and so the judge let him go. I suspect there have been others, but Kate is the only one I ever heard of.'

Smokey shook his head. 'Hard to figure,' he said, 'something like that happening. I mean a woman and all.'

The men sat thinking about it. After a while Louie, obviously thinking about where they were and why, came up with a question. 'Wonder what the fella what got hung here was planning on doing?' he asked. 'Smokey, what's the country like up in those foothills to the south?'

'Uh, just more rolling grasslands mostly. There's a few little outfits on another ten miles or so, but things seem to be a bit dryer out that way. Not really good cattle country.'

'Well,' Buck said, 'guess we'll take a

look around here come daylight. Maybe there's enough sign to show what that fella was up to. From what I could see coming in, this here looks good. Kinda hidden off the trail where a jag could be kept out of sight while a running iron could be made hot enough.'

Smokey nodded. 'I didn't spend much time. Just wanted to cut him down and get him off that tree limb. The only thing I saw I can really remember was that blackened cinch ring.'

'That's all a man needs,' said Buck, 'if'n he's any good. Someone knows how to go about it can take a cinch ring, build a fire to get it hot and make nearly any brand you'd want.'

'Wal,' said Louie, 'I heard a story about that once. About a fella what used a saddle cinch ring as a running iron. He was caught with a small herd all branded with a big 48. Claimed that was his brand. The men who caught him didn't believe him so they shot one of the branded steers and peeled back the hide.

'As you might figure, brands take a while to heal. On the animal's flesh the Bar S had been branded. Clear as you'd want, the Bar S with the numbers four and eight over it.'

Taking a stick Louie marked out Bar S in the dirt. Using the line of the 'bar' he added little lines making it the number 4. The letter 'S' was quickly made into an '8'.

'Anyway that satisfied the men they had a rustler and strung him up.'

'Hmm,' said Buck pensively, 'I've heard of men using twists of wire, too. Altering brands is a frequent practice among rustlers.'

'Uh huh,' said Louie, yawning, 'but just like with most men who think it's easier to make a living stealing from others, rustlers all too often end up working harder than anyone trying to make an honest living. I always thought people like that weren't the smartest frogs in the pond.'

32

Sleep came easy for the men that night. Whether it was all that fresh air, the long ride the day before or just becoming relaxed around the slowly dying camp-fire. For all of that though Louie was up and around, had the fire built up and coffee brewing when Buck rolled out of his blankets. Hearing the men talking woke Smokey up.

'Tell you what Smokey,' said Buck after blowing to cool his cup of coffee, 'we get breakfast out of the way and I'll help you load up your supplies. No reason you can't go on doing whatever it was you'd come out this way for. Louie and I will likely spend a couple hours looking the place over then head back toward town.'

'Sounds good. The line shack is on over the next little ridge or two. It'll probably take me the rest of the day to unload and get the cabin cleaned out. It don't take them damn packrats long to start abuilding their nests once the hands get shot of the place. I always figure to spend at least a day cleaning, fixing and stacking up some firewood. Won't be long before a crew'll be coming out to make a gather.'

Louie looked up from the frying pan sizzling with thick slices of bacon. 'Country looks like it could get a little rough. Lots of these little canyons and gullies. Wouldn't want the job of chousing them longhorns out of the brush. I worked a couple years for a spread down on the Texas-Louisiana border. Country a lot like this. Getting the bulls out of the brush was bad enough, but when it came to the cows, especially if'n they got young stuff suckling, well, watch out. There were times I thought blasting powder woulda been the best thing to have.'

'Yeah. I started working for Mr Jacobson about five years ago. The first couple years I and another young cowhand worked at keeping the horse stock ready. Then that fella, Price, he came into the area and started breaking saddle stock. The next gather I was out there with the rest of the hands, yelling and roping and getting the crap scared outa me. Nothing much worse than a mama cow or one of them big old steers what don't want to leave the scrub brush.'

'Many head get used to finding a home up in this hill country?' asked Buck, using a piece of dried-hard bread to mop up the bacon drippings from his tin plate.

'Oh, not all that many. We'll likely get a couple hundred head outa the brush. Won't take long to cut out the yearlings and slap a brand on them. Those are the ones we'll drive down closer to the main ranch. Put them all together with what's out on the flats for a major drive to the railhead.'

Louie nodded. 'Sounds like a lot of hard work. Think I'll stick with doing what we're doing, jobs here and there nobody else wants to do.'

The sun wasn't much more than an hour or so above the horizon when, after helping the young hand tie his supplies onto the pack horse, Buck was watching him ride out of sight. Riding the big black horse to the top of a nearby ridge he sat for a while rolling a quirley, looking out over the range.

From where he sat he had a good view down a long, wide ravine thick with brush and scruffy-looking meadows. A line of low-lying trees meandered down marking a small creek. Moving his horse to where it could chomp grass from another little patch, he found himself looking into yet another draw. He couldn't see any water and the brush was a lot thinner and coarser.

Shaking his head, Buck reined around and rode back into the gully they'd camped in.

'That Smokey get gone?' asked Louie.

'Yeah. Thinking about the work of

pulling ornery old cattle out of the brush like he'll be doing soon doesn't appeal to me.'

Louie chuckled. 'Won't bother him. He's still young. Now you and me, well, never mind.'

'I took a little ride up that ridge on over there.' Buck lifted a thumb to give a direction. 'About the first of a series of hills from what I could see. We're far enough from the mountains that the trees covering them looked blue-green. I couldn't see very far but from what I could tell there are a lot of ravines and arroyos in this part of the Frying Pan range. Hard country to work in, that's for sure.'

Louie only nodded. 'While you was taking it easy with a morning walk I went down to look over where the rustler had been working. Found the fire-blackened cinch ring Smokey talked about. Cold dead ashes from a bit of a fire, but not much else.'

'Uh huh. Well, my little ride was kinda interesting. You know, from where

I was setting up there, I couldn't see one steer. Not one animal anywhere. Now it's still early and this is the time of day most cows will want to head for water. Didn't see anything moving any place.'

'Well, I never thought about it, but I can't recall seeing much stock coming up. Not since we left the flat lands anyhow,' he stopped, thinking. 'You know, now that you mention it, there's something else I just thought of. That fella Smokey brought into town. The rustler. Wasn't he supposed to have been using that cinch ring for a running iron to change brands?' Buck nodded. 'Well, there wasn't one sign of there having been any cattle anywhere in that little swale. Oh, there's one of them narrow little trails livestock and deer use threading through the brush. But no cow pies or chomped down grass like there would have been if that rustler was working on more'n one critter at a time. I don't think that fella was really doing anything that should get him hung up in that tree.'

33

Riding away later in the morning, both men kept an eye on the range. Neither said anything but both remembered having been ambushed not so long back. At one point, about an hour after leaving the foothills where they'd spent the night, they spotted a small bunch of cattle spread across a grassy slope. Louie pointed them out to his saddle partner.

'Wonder if we were to go riding that way what brand we'd find on those critters. They're about the closest of any we've seen since leaving that branding fire and running iron.'

'Ah, they'd most likely have been branded with the Frying Pan iron. But it's not likely we'd get close enough to read any brands. Longhorns are especially spooky after being a long time away from any riders. Shorthorns, on the other hand, don't seem to care.'

'Uh huh. I notice the way we're headed, I'd say we'll be paying the Frying Pan another visit. You reckon we'll find answers to anything there we didn't get the last time? What you got buzzing around in that head of yours?'

'Yeah. Well I've been thinking about not seeing any sign of cattle back near the rustler's fire. Thought it'd be a good idea to find out more about young Smokey.'

'Ya think he wasn't telling it true?'

'Don't know. Just thought it might be worthwhile. Why, you got a hot date back in Auburn I don't know about?'

'Don't I wish. The mayor's daughter, now, she's a looker. Awfully young but awfully fun to watch. Must be my Mexican blood acting up. Us Mexicans are all great lovers, ya know.'

Buck laughed. 'No, I didn't know. Haven't seen much sign of it lately either. Look there,' he pointed off to the side. 'That's a pretty big bunch of cattle spread out over there. Must be getting close to the home ranch. According to Smokey the hands will be somewhere up in this part of the ranch beating the brush for marketable cattle. I expect they'll chase them down to these lowlands for branding.'

The Frying Pan range was big; it took another two hours riding or more before the main ranch buildings came into sight.

'I wonder what kind of reception we'll get this time,' muttered Louie as they rode into the ranch yard, 'what with the young firebrand back there somewhere.'

'Know soon enough. There's the bossman up on the front veranda watching us ride in.' Pulling up at the hitchrail Buck nodded and called out, 'Good morning, Mr Jacobson. Would appreciate a few minutes of your time.'

'Wal, come on up outa the sunshine.' Stepping back to an open door he called out, 'Hey, Mirella. Got a couple saddle-bums riding in looking for coffee. Got any of this morning's left over?' Turning back he laughed, 'C'mon up, gents. If I know Mirella, and I do, she'll be out in a bit with fresh coffee and likely pieces from that apple pie she's been working on. Give those horses of yours a break and c'mon up.'

Shaking the man's hand, Buck smiled. 'Well, if we had known there was apple pie waiting to be sampled we'd've been here earlier. Thank you.'

Jacobson chuckled. 'That woman is a jewel. Loves to bake and turns out some of the best bear-claws, pies and cakes you've ever tasted. Why, I swear, I could cut the hands' pay in half and we'd still get all the help needed just cause of her baking.'

'It's one of your hands we'd like to talk to you about.'

'Oh? What'd one of them do, try to chase you off the place as you rode in? That ain't like them.'

'No.' Buck shook his head, and then stopped when the woman came out carrying a coffee pot and cups.

'The pie is just out of the oven,' she

said. 'It should cool down a bit before I cut into it.'

Buck waited until she went back into the house.

'Naw, we didn't see anyone riding in. Passed by a lot of cattle but no hired hands. No, it's the one called Smokey we'd like to know more about.'

'Hmm, now that doesn't surprise me. He brought that dead man into town didn't he? Said he found him hanging out along the south section. He brought him here and I sent him on into town. Figured you'd want to know about it.'

'Oh, yeah, he came in yesterday packing the body. He said he was headed out to supply a line shack, out near where he found the man hanging. We rode out with him. Wanted to see if there was anything we could find might lead up to the vigilantes.'

'Yeah? Well, it's likely the fella Smokey found was left there by that damn Vigilance Committee. You two getting any closer to finding out who's in that gang?'

Buck shook his head. 'Afraid not. Not by name, anyhow. We have learned a few things, though. Bits and pieces of things. I figure we get a few more and we'll have something to work with. But for now, nothing taking us to naming any of them.'

'So what can I help you with then? Didn't the youngster tell you all about what he'd found?'

'Oh, yeah,' said Buck, 'he told us all about it there in town. The sheriff and a couple other men heard too. Then the three of us rode out to where he'd made his grisly discovery. Left the body for the undertaker to take care of. Sheriff McDonald said he thought he could get the business owners to share the cost of burying the man.'

'Yeah, guess Smokey thought I'd want to plant him up in the ranch burying ground. But I thought it was better to take him into town.'

'No, what we wanted to do was get to know a bit more about Smokey. Young — but from what he said we got the idea he was a good hand. Said he'd hired on only a few years ago.'

Jacobson nodded. 'Yeah. Came riding in one morning. Green as grass, he was. Knew how to sit a saddle but didn't know beans about cattle. I put him onto working with another fella, Ivan Espinosa. Another youngster. His pa was a German settler from down around the border country. Ma was Mexican. Anyway Ivan has a good touch with our riding stock. Smokey, he was known as Horace Grant then. Changed his name one day after buying a six-gun in a slick holster. Ah, the pie!' he exclaimed as Mirella brought out the sweet-smelling pie, forks and plates.

All talk ceased as the three men ate large pieces of the still-warm apple pie. Washing it down with more coffee, they sat back satisfied.

'Now that,' said Louie wiping a crumb from his lower lip, 'was enough to make me think about changing jobs. But then if I was to have as much as I'd like, for sure I'd get too big for any horse to carry me. That was a wonderful treat. She ducked back into the house before I could tell her how great it was. Let her know, will you?'

Jacobson chuckled proudly. 'I sure will. And you're right. Getting fat here is a worry, what with Mirella's cooking.'

Nothing was said for a moment, then the rancher nodded. 'Yeah, soon as he strapped on that fancy gun rig he somehow changed. Don't know what it was, but, well, it was like he suddenly grew up. Only,' he hesitated, 'he didn't really. You know what I mean?'

'What was there about the six-gun that caused that?' asked Buck.

'Don't know for sure. He bought the rig, a wide leather gunbelt and holster all carved with curlicues and things, and a Colt Dragoon like that one you're wearing. Saved his money and bought it in town. Story was a half-dozen soldiers came riding in with two bodies draped over a couple horses. Asked if the two could be buried. Offered to pay for it with the horses and gear owned by the two dead men. The pair had been wanted up in Colorado Territory and the US Army was sent to bring them in. Anyhow, it was one of the dead men who'd owned the fancy gun rig that Horace bought. Wasn't long before he told everyone he was changing his name to Smokey. Seemed like a kid thing to do, but it's what he wanted. Musta been something bad about the gun rig, you reckon?'

34

Louie frowned and shook his head. 'I have never heard about a gun causing trouble. The person pulling the trigger, yeah. Lots of times. But not the gun.'

'What had the two dead men done to get the army to chase them down? Did the soldier boys say?' asked Buck.

'Well, according to what one of those fellers said after a few drinks in the saloon, they were the leaders of a gang up north. Felipe and Guillermo Jimenez by name. Brothers, originally from Vera Cruz, Mexico. According to the story, they had apparently seen their family killed when the town was shelled during the Mexican-American War. After the end of that war the Spanish land grant their family had had was not honoured by the Americans, who sold the land off to white settlers. The brothers were young and had lost everything. They and others like them took to stealing and rustling from the settlers.

'Chased north, the gang robbed and murdered all along the way, ending up in Bent's Fort, a small town in the Colorado Territory. Things got so bad with the gang nearly taking over the town the US Cavalry was called in. In a big gun battle, most of the gang members were caught with only the brothers escaping. The army turned the men they'd captured over to the folks in Bent's Fort and they were quickly hung. The brothers were tracked down by the cavalry, finally caught outside of Auburn. The gun belt and Colt Horace bought had belonged to one of the brothers.'

The men sat quiet for a time, thinking about the story.

Finally Buck broke the silence. 'I've heard a lot of stories of terrible things happening in that war and in the one right after it, the War of Rebellion or Civil War, as some call it. Like Louie said though, never heard anyone blaming the bad things on guns. Or about guns changing a man's behaviour.'

'Maybe,' said Jacobson. 'He'd had a pistol before getting old Samuel Colt's pride and joy. Was an old cap-and-ball Navy. He said it'd belonged to his pa. In all the time he's been on the place that's about all what's ever been said about his past. When he came riding in hunting work, he had a pair of worn saddlebags hanging from an old scratched saddle. Everything he owned was packed in those bags, and let me tell you, they weren't packing a lot. The horse? Well, poor animal was turned out and died some little bit later. But that pistol he carried in his pocket. You know how most hands carry a rifle and lots a hand gun. Never know when you gotta kill a varmint or an injured animal. That's what happened with Smokey back before he changed his name. Was out somewhere by hisself when his horse stepped in a gopher hole. Broke a leg. He said the bone was white, showing through the hide. Well, the horse couldn't walk and there wasn't nothing to do but he had to shoot it. His pistol was a smaller caliber and it took three shots to the head to do her. Tore the youngster up, it did.'

'Yeah,' said Louie quietly, 'I knew a man carried an old Navy Colt. Think it was only a .36 caliber. That's not a very big piece of lead.'

'Well, that's his story. Bought a bigger Colt, changed his name and has grown into being a pretty good hand. Now, what exactly happened that made you want to know about him?'

Buck thought about it then nodded. 'His story is he was riding out to some line shack when a bunch of crows making a racket somewhere off in the bush caught his attention. He rode into a little ravine and found the man hanging. Ashes from a small fire and a blackened cinch ring nearby. Obviously a rustler. Except when we rode out there looking, we noticed there was no sign of any cattle having been penned up waiting to be branded. No cattle anywhere, no cow pats, no nothing. Makes us wonder.'

Jacobson looked down at the porch floor. 'I don't know,' he said, 'the kid's been a good worker. Rarely causes any trouble, least ways didn't until he got that damn gun rig. I still don't have any real reason to think differently. Just don't know what to tell you.'

'Well,' said Buck, 'I guess there isn't really much to say. It just didn't look right. Guess there could be good reason for it to be like that, but,' he shrugged, 'don't know what it'd be.'

'So what do you want me to do?'

'Nothing. He did a good job, bringing in the dead man. And with other than that little bit of bother, his story makes sense. I wouldn't trouble him about it.'

Thanking the rancher for his time and the pie, the two rode on, wanting to make it to town before dark.

Riding over the bridge just outside of town, the two pulled up and sat for a moment looking down into the moving water. The sun had just gone down and the surface of the river was dark, broken only when a fish jumped for some insect.

'Well, at least there aren't any bodies hanging around waiting for us,' said Louie.

'Didn't someone say the Committee had used this bridge a couple times? You know, that was something else missing on the man Smokey brought in, the Committee hadn't left a note pinned to his shirt.'

'Ya don't think there could be more'n one bunch of hangmen wandering around, do ya?'

'No reason to think so. Darn it, don't mention anything like that to the sheriff or Winterbottom. They've got enough to worry about.'

'Yeah. OK, let's get going. Might still be able to get some supper before the cook closes up for the night.'

35

Breakfast the next morning was beef steak and eggs. Buck looked at the inch-thick steak taking up most of the plate in front of Louie and snorted.

'You sure like to make it easy on the cook back there, don't you?'

'What do ya mean?'

'Look at that piece of dead cow you've got. Cookie only had to cut it off the carcass hanging in the cool room, wave it over the fire and slap it onto the plate. Quick and easy. Why, it isn't far from still breathing.'

'Well, I do like my beef cooked right, black on the outside and red inside. All the flavour of the one you're cutting up has been burned out.'

Buck chuckled. 'I gotta admit, your breakfast is colourful — blood red beef, white and yellow eggs. Almost patriotic.'

Louie slapped the bottom of the ketchup bottle, trying to get the sauce to pour. 'Well, maybe,' he said, not looking up from his meal, 'for sure it's enough to keep me going through the first half of the day. Colourful or not.' Wiping the bit of grease from his chin, he looked up at his partner. 'What're we up to today? Far as I can see we aren't much closer to earning the money than we were riding into this town.'

'Well, yes, I have to admit there's a lot we don't know. But I've got a hunch something will break directly. All that riding around just might have stirred something up.'

'Uh huh. Might. But then again might not.'

The same questions came up again a little later. Sitting in the chairs on the hotel porch, to let their breakfast settle according to Louie, they watched the town mayor and sheriff come down the street.

'Well, Buck,' said Louie quietly, 'here

come the paymasters, wanting to know what we've found out. Hope they can handle disappointment.'

'Old son, you sure are depressing today. Must be that hunk of raw meat setting in your stomach.' Looking up he greeted the two officials. 'Good morning gents. Out checking to see how the town is faring this morning?'

'Nope,' said Mayor Winterbottom, 'just wondering what you found out on your ride yesterday.'

Buck smiled. 'Not much, really. It was much like that rider, Smokey, said. The tree he'd found the rustler hanging from was a bit down in a shallow ravine. Ashes from a small fire and right close by a fire-blackened cinch ring. Everything just as he said. Came away with a couple questions, though. I haven't figured it out yet, but a few things about the set-up bothered me.'

Sheriff McDonald settled in a chair and turned to face the two men. 'Something didn't look right? That young cowboy miss something?'

'No, from what we could see he told it about right. But there's something. How about the jasper he brought in, find out anything about who he was?'

'Nope. Nothing in his pockets. Hell, he was wearing just about what everyone riding around on horseback would have. Run-down boots, denim pants and threadbare shirt. Now what did you find out there that bothers you?'

Buck frowned. 'Not much really, just a couple things that don't feel right. For instance, we didn't find a hat anywhere near where he'd been strung up. How many men riding anywhere are going bare-headed? Look at us sitting here, all four of us have hats of one kind or another. Smokey didn't bring one in with the body and we didn't find one out there either. So, where is it and what happened to it?'

Winterbottom and the sheriff both looked serious.

'And no gun belt,' said Buck. 'Fact is, no sign the fellow had even been armed. Can't say he didn't have a rifle shoved in a saddle rig cause there was no sign of his even having a horse. Smokey used his ranch pack horse to bring him in, remember?'

'Yeah, I didn't think of that,' said McDonald. 'Never crossed my mind.'

'What are you saying?' asked Winterbottom. 'That Smokey's got something to do with it? You think he's part of the Committee?'

'Not saying anything. I just don't know. As I said, a couple things bother me. On the way back to town we stopped at the Frying Pan to have another talk with Jacobson. Smokey had gone on, taking the supplies out to one of the ranch line shacks. I wanted to know more about the young hand. According to the rancher, Smokey is a good man. Does his job and doesn't cause much trouble with the rest of the hands. Right now all I can say is, I just don't know.'

The four men were silent, thinking. Finally Winterbottom, shaking his head, grunted. 'Well, I certainly don't have any answers. We got us a dead man to bury, a man who could have been a rustler or maybe not. I had that young newspaper fellow asking me about the dead one and didn't have any answers for him. That's going to look good in the paper, isn't it? The only positive he'd been able to report is that we hired someone to come in and investigate. Since then there's been two more hangings, one right outside town, for God's sake. Those folks back there considering the statehood deal must be having second thoughts. I don't know what to do.' After another minute with no one having anything to offer, he stood up. 'Guess I'll open up the store. Matty's sleeping in this morning. Haven't seen much of her the last couple days. Don't know what's keeping her busy, but, well, guess that's part of growing up. Ah, well, not much else to do, sweep out the place and hope nobody brings in any more dead men.'

The men sat for a while, watching a

few riders and one wagon came into town. The horsemen, nodding to the sheriff as they rode by, stopped to tie up at Winterbottom's store. The wagon went on down the street disappearing around the corner of the huge livery barn.

'I could go fishing,' said McDonald after a bit, 'haven't much else to do. You two have any plans for the day?'

'No,' said Buck, 'all I've got are questions. Don't know where to go to find answers, though. I hate to just do nothing, waiting for something to happen, someone to make a mistake. But to tell the truth, I don't know what else to do. Like the mayor says, hope nobody finds another rustler to hang.'

36

As the morning sun rose high enough to make the shadows of the buildings across the street stand out, Buck and Louie shifted their chairs down out of direct sunlight. Slowly traffic along the main street picked up a little, giving the two men something to focus on. After an hour or so even that was starting to pall.

'As I recall,' said Louie, 'the last time I went to get coffee. Now I could be wrong, but . . . '

'Yeah, you could be. However, as I'm such a nice person, and because sitting here is getting boring, I'll volunteer to do the heavy work.'

Chuckling, he walked down the street to the restaurant. Coming back a few minutes later he saw that Louie was no longer on the porch. *Must have gone to the outhouse*, Buck thought, smiling.

Making room for more coffee, I'll wager.

Settling down he sipped his coffee and propped his boot heels up on the porch railing. There had been times when he could take comfort in doing nothing but they were usually few and far between. Somehow, time to merely relax and enjoy the morning was rare.

Thinking those thoughts and enjoying the moment, he was slightly annoyed when a boy came running up the boardwalk.

'Hey mister, your big horse just tried to bite a man. He did. Wasn't bit, though. The man jumped away and said some pretty bad words.'

'Who was the man, son? The old fellow at the livery stable?'

'No. I don't know who he is. He and a couple others were helping your partner onto his own horse. Your partner looked like he was drunk. And it ain't even noon yet.'

Buck sat up. 'Wait a minute. What are you saying? Someone was putting Louie on the back of his horse?'

'Yeah. They were trying to put a saddle on your horse, that's when it tried to bite the man. Couldn't do that so they threw a saddle on another one. I was watching. Supposed to be at school but I was hiding behind a bale of hay.'

'They put Louie on a horse? How many were there?'

'Oh, three I think. Yeah. Three of them. Huh, maybe four. They rode out the back of the stable and went around that way.' He pointed.

Tossing his coffee into the street, Buck dropped the cup onto his chair. 'Thanks, son. I'd better go see what's happening.'

It had to be the Committee. They had come in and got Louie. Had to be. Only thing that made sense. They were going to string him up.

Wearing high-heeled riding boots, Buck didn't like running. But not liking what the boy had said, he ran down the street. Inside the stable was dark and empty. No sign of anyone. Through to the corral in back, he looked in the direction the boy had indicated. Nothing.

His stud horse had come to the railing when Buck came out. Buck pulled the horse inside and quickly threw on his saddle. Before climbing on board he dug into the saddlebag and pulled out his extra Colt. Sticking it behind his belt in back, he swung up.

The big black horse must have caught the rider's anxiety or maybe it was the heel drumming against its flanks but when the horse came out of the barn, it was running full out.

The bridge. They'd taken Louie around back. The thoughts were going through Buck's mind as fast as the horse was running. They'd go to the bridge. Bending low he raced down the street and out of town.

37

Foamy sweat was flicked off the black's neck when looking ahead, Buck saw men standing on the bridge close to one side. Not hesitating, he pulled his Colt and fired. Too far to hit anything, he just wanted them to know he was coming. Shooting high so as not to hit Louie, he fired off a couple more shots.

The bunch on the bridge broke up, running off the other way. Buck slid the horse to a halt, out of the saddle before the animal had stopped. Glancing to the only man left standing he saw it was Louie, trussed up with a noose hanging around his neck.

Standing straight with his gun at arm's length, Buck aimed at the running men who had reached their horses and were swinging into the saddle. Squeezing the trigger, Buck saw one rider jerk to one side. Grabbing the saddle horn on the running horse, the wounded man fled. Quickly shifting his aim Buck got off another shot. The bullet must have hit the horse as the front of the animal crumbled, throwing the rider head-first to the ground.

Not seeing any other targets, Buck rushed toward Louie to rip the noose away.

'Hold up there,' someone yelled as a slug tore at the bridge plank near Buck's feet.

Buck swung around to see a man coming at him from the end of the bridge. Isaac Black, his gun pointing, laughing.

'Wal, ain't this pretty?' he called, stopping and holding his six-gun swinging from Buck to Louie. 'I got me a couple rangers. Yes sir. And won't old Fitz be paying me extra for this? You better believe it.'

Buck stood, his Colt as his side. 'What do you mean, Fitz paying extra?'

'Oh, hell, you don't know nothing do ya? Hoo boy, now that's something.'

'It's clear you're part of the Vigilance Committee.'

Black laughed loudly. 'Part of it? Hell no, we are it. All the time you was thinking there was a gang when it was just a couple of us. That's all it took. Not a gang. Boy, does that make you look foolish. We was laughing every time we heard you was looking for a gang.'

'And what does Fitzwalter have to do with it?'

'More showing how dumb you are. It was Fitz who's been behind it all the time. It was his idea and it's him been paying us to do the dirty work. And now, when I shoot you and kick your Mexican partner off the bridge there'll be a bonus. Ha! I told you I'd be shooting you, didn't I?'

Buck shook his head. 'Not while I'm still standing, you won't.'

'Oh, yes. What could be better. Ya did some fancy shooting coming to stop us, but think about it. I'm betting your six gun is plumb empty. Yup, I'll take my time and do you with one shot then come kick your pard all the way to hell.'

Buck turned his head as if glancing down at his pistol but his eyes never left the other man. Black, laughing, followed his glance. That was all Buck needed. While Black had been talking Buck had been slowly reaching around with his left hand to the Colt behind his belt. When Black looked down, Buck came around with his extra gun and shot the man in the chest. Twice.

Black staggered back a step or two, looking down at his body then crumbling.

Buck lifted the noose from Louie's neck and using his pocket knife, cut his hands free.

'Boy, you sure took your time,' Louie complained. 'I didn't think you were ever going to get here.'

'Oh, stop your bitching. I got here as fast as I could. Had to finish my coffee, didn't I? Anyway, who went for a ride with that bunch? Me or you? How'd that happen, anyhow?'

'Ah hell. It was that Winterbottom girl. Came asking if I'd help her. So of course I did. And they were waiting.'

'Of course you did,' said Buck cutting Louie's feet loose. Then looking down where the horse had fallen, he frowned. 'C'mon,' he said and took off running.

The horse was dead. Buck could see where his bullet had struck the animal in the head. Rushing over to where the rider lay in a heap, he saw it was Mathilda Winterbottom. Feeling her neck, he felt a weak pulse.

'Louie,' he called, 'she's still alive. Bring my horse down. We'll get her back into town to the doctor.'

38

Buck carried the girl to the doctor's office while Louie went to the store to get her father. She was still unconscious and Buck was told to go away. He was going out the door as Winterbottom came running in.

Outside, he found Louie talking to the sheriff. Slowly taking it all in, Sheriff McDonald could only shake his head.

'You really think she was part of the gang?'

'Wasn't any gang,' said Buck. 'According to Black, it was just a couple of them. And,' thinking ahead, he glanced at Louie before going on, 'I don't really think Mathilda had much to do with them. Not with the hangings. Look at it, she's young, a girl just coming on to being a woman and that Isaac Black must have looked like something to her. Now yes, she did get my partner to go help her, but you have to remember, he's a Mexican and they are all great lovers, ya know? As far as her being part of the Vigilance Committee? I'd say no.'

'Louie said Black claims Fitzwalter was behind it. That I can believe. He somehow never did fit in here. I can see how Jacobson or Runkle would have reason for doing something like that, but Fitzwalter? His little horse operation isn't big enough for that.'

Buck shook his head. 'And you're probably right. But remember what that marshal told us. You recall he came over to tell you to keep an eye out for a real bad man — uh, can't remember his name. Didn't he say that outlaw and Fitzwalter had known each other sometime in the past? Well, what if the horse ranch he's got is really just a place outlaws could hide out? For a price. If so, then Fitzwalter would have as big a reason as the other ranchers to stop any statehood talk.'

'Um, maybe. Guess I'd better telegraph the marshal, let him know what's been happening and what Fitzwalter might be up to.'

'Might think about getting someone to drag Mathilda's horse off the road too. Oh, and bring in Black's body. Personally I'd be for leaving it out there to rot, but with the stage coming by once in a while might not be a good idea.'

39

The rest of the afternoon was spent hanging around waiting for Mathilda to regain consciousness. By nightfall the doctor could only report that her condition hadn't changed. He joined the sheriff, Buck and Louie at the saloon for a drink before going back to his office.

'Her father is there now,' explained Doctor Bass. 'He hasn't left her side. Keeps looking up at me as if there might be something I should be doing. There isn't. She must have landed on her head when her horse went down. Suffering from a concussion, I'd say. There's not much can be done except wait. She's a young woman and pretty strong. All we can do is wait and let her sleep.'

After the doctor had left, the others sat around sipping their drinks. Having talked what had happened into the ground they soon found themselves with little to say. Finishing his glass of beer, Buck wished them a good night and left. Louie wasn't far behind.

Sheriff McDonald joined Louie and Buck at breakfast the next morning, saying nothing had changed with Mathilda overnight. There wasn't much talk while the men ate their pancakes, sausage, eggs and slices of toasted homemade bread. They were relaxing over their coffee when a man came into the restaurant.

'Why, it isn't Saturday, Mr Jacobson,' said Sheriff McDonald. 'Not usual seeing you in town middle of the week.'

'Nope, and don't think I want to be here, either. I came in early hoping you'd be offering me some breakfast.'

'Ah, no. Sorry, but we just finished. You been here an hour or so back, well, maybe. But . . . '

Jacobson chuckled. 'Oh well, can't have everything.' Looking at first Buck then Louie, he sobered. 'Course, the reason I came in was to talk to you two. You were showing a lot of interest in one of my men — Smokey?'

Both Buck and Louie nodded but didn't say anything.

'Well, he's dead. Came riding in yesterday afternoon all stretched out over his saddle, barely hanging on, all bloody. Been shot in the shoulder. By the time he got to the ranch he'd about bled out, was weak and breathing shallow. Me'n Mirella laid him out and washed up his wound. The bullet had taken him from the back, shattered that big bone and tore a hole you could nearly walk through coming out. He never woke up. Died a couple hours later. Now I don't know where he'd been or what he'd been doing. I know where he was supposed to be, but it wasn't any place he'd likely get shot. So I came in to find out if y'all knew anything.'

He stopped, waiting. Buck thought about it a minute then explained. 'I was the one who shot him, Mr Jacobson.'

And went on to explain what had happened and what his hired hand had been doing.

'Well, I can say it isn't surprising. No, don't get me wrong. If'n I'd have known, I'd have sent him packing. But, well, he's changed in recent times. Been something not exactly right since he got most of his growth. Hearing he'd been part of the vigilantes doesn't surprise me. Too bad, he was a good hand and a likable young man to boot. But you can't never tell, can you?'

After the waitress filled their cups for the third or fourth time, the men sat quietly, thinking about what had gone on. It was then Winterbottom came pushing through the door. Scowling, the mayor came over to the table and threw down a packet of money in front of Buck.

'There,' he said snarling, 'that's the money owed you. Now you've been paid so you don't have to stay around.' Not taking his gaze off Buck, he went on. 'Matty just died. She never came awake, never said a word. You, mister, killed my daughter. You got your money, you've done your job. Now get out of my town. Get out of my sight.'

40

Sheriff McDonald followed the two out of the restaurant and stood for a moment on the boardwalk.

'Boys, I don't know what to tell you. Will isn't himself since his daughter started acting up. I've known him since, well, since he arrived in town. Even then, taking over the general store and then becoming our mayor, even his keeping involved, everything came after his daughter. Well, hell, you know how it is with youngsters. They get to a certain age and think there ain't nothing they don't know or can't handle. Matty wasn't no different. She wasn't a child when they got here but she was still polite and hard working. Always there when Will had to do something; being mayor took him outa the store and Matty'd take care of business. I don't know when it happened but things changed. It was a slow change, but here this past year or so she wasn't somehow so polite. I don't know. Her pa didn't either. He was getting to his wits' end, watching her carrying on. I guess what I'm trying to say, is don't let his anger bother you. He's just lost the centre of his life and needs someone to blame. You're handy.'

Buck nodded. 'Finding out what she's been doing behind his back has got to be painful. Having her die, I can understand the pain he's got. Well, maybe not really understand it, but . . . Anyway, don't worry about it.' Glancing at Louie, he looked back at the lawman. Smiling he shook hands with McDonald. 'I reckon he's right though. Louie and me, we've done what we came here to do. No reason for us to hang around. Would only be a burr in his side, renewing the pain every time he saw us. We've been paid off, so I'd say it was time to be travelling.'

'Well, that's probably best. But don't go away thinking we don't appreciate what you've done for us.'

Louie smiled and nodded. 'Yeah. Now the newspapers can let the big guns back in Washington, D.C. know that the territory is safe to become a state. Your little town will grow because of it and maybe your mayor will be too busy to dwell on his loss.'

41

Saddling up, Buck tied down his saddlebags. 'Not much food stuff in there,' he said, patting the leather pouches. 'I don't reckon we should wait for the mayor to open up to store to stock up. Guess we'll have to wait until we get to the next town.'

'That's not a worry,' said Louie swinging into the saddle. 'We can be over in Fort Rawlins by supper time if we don't dawdle around. That's about the closest place to load up.'

Buck nodded.

Riding out of town, neither looked back. 'What have you got in mind?' asked Louie as they neared the bridge. 'Any idea of where we're going? That money we were paid will take care of things for a while but sooner or later we're going to have to look up some work.'

'Uh huh,' said Buck slowly, 'but you know we didn't completely wrap up what we'd been paid to do. Fitzwalter was the organizer of the Committee and all we did was take that away from him. I'm thinking we're not done here.'

'Huh. Any chance you're thinking about Yarberry?'

'Well, he did say he was going to shoot us, only when it was the right time to do it. I can't see any sense in letting that ride, not knowing if or when he'll be coming. Nope, I'd say we still got a few things to do.'

Mention of Yarberry made them once again pay close attention to the land they were riding through. Buck didn't say anything but he'd been thinking. Remembering the time it took them to ride from the Mustang Ranch into town, he figured they would be well past the horse ranch by late afternoon. From what they'd been told the stage road curved around the end of the mountain range.

'We've got coffee and a couple cans

of beans,' he said at one point. 'I'm thinking we'll turn off the stage road once we're past Fitzwalter's place. Find ourselves a place to hunker down for the night up in the foothills above the main ranch.'

'That bad man the territorial marshal came over to talk about, he might be there at Fitzwalter's place too. Shouldn't ought to forget him.'

'Wasn't. The good news is there'll only be two of them. I don't count on the dude, Fitzwalter, for much. With Black out of the way there's likely to be only the two to worry about.'

Finding a long, shallow gully angling back up into the foothills, the two men reined off the roadway. For another hour or so they rode, keeping off any high ridges, holding the horses to a steady walk. Riding through the scrubby manzanita brush and stunted pines and pin oaks meant following random game trails, always keeping to a southerly direction. The gully itself deepened into a wider ravine as they went along. Slowly the floor of the low ravine had gained in elevation until coming to the end of it, up and over a little rise they came onto a wider trail. While in the low ravine, the sun had gone behind the higher hills. Riding up the slope, they found themselves back in sunlight.

'Think this could be the trail they talked about?' asked Louie. 'Coming over from Fort Rawlins?'

Sitting their saddles and inspecting the trail, Buck nodded.

'Not much horse traffic, from what I can see. Those horse droppings over there look to have dried out. Say a few days anyhow. Yeah, I'd guess this is it.'

'So which way, on up a ways to look for a camp place, or back down the way we came?'

'Up. If anyone should ride along here they'd be less likely to smell smoke if our fire was higher. Riders don't usually pay much attention to what's above them either.'

'Well, after being ambushed, I gotta say, I sure do.'

Supper, a couple cans of beans heated by a small fire and coffee brewed in their fire-blackened pot, was over quickly. Smothering the fire, they spread their bed rolls off near a huge boulder on what looked like a soft place. The horses, hobbled, nibbled at a patch of scrub grass nearby.

Up with the sun, they quickly threw together a little fire and for breakfast heated the left-over coffee.

'What do you have in mind?' asked Louie as they saddled their horses.

'Haven't got much of a plan. Just ride on until we can see what's there. Hide out and maybe see what we're up against. I figure we can leave once Yarberry and Fitzwalter are taken care of. That other fellow too. Probably be a good idea to see how many hands there are. After we get all that figured out is when we can make a plan. Basically I suppose it's going to be simply surprise them and hit 'em hard.'

42

Riding the trail they'd come up on, they made their way down toward the valley. Still riding through brush there was little chance they could be seen from very far away. At one point, coming up a low rise they found themselves looking down on the back of a big barn.

'Guess that's it,' said Buck, and reined back behind a clump of trees. 'We can leave the horses here and go see what's what.' Taking his extra six-gun from the saddle-bag, he once again shoved it behind his belt.

A door at the back of the barn had been hung on leather straps. Slowly pulling it open, they eased inside. The planks used in the construction of the barn had been green and after years of drying in the sun, there were large gaps between them. If the barn had ever been chinked the mud had dried and fallen out. Sunlight filtering through those gaps cut the shadows. Other than bales of hay stacked along one side, the barn was empty.

Walking with his revolver held along his leg, Buck went to the front. Looking through an opening between the planks he could see the cabin across the yard. A huge tree off to one side shaded part of it. Smoke lifted lazily from a stove pipe atop the cabin.

'There's a bunch standing around a corral,' Louie said quietly. He had gone to one side and was bending down to look out through a gap. 'Looks like four men leaning against a corral rail watching what was happening inside.'

Buck went over. 'Nothing moving over at the cabin,' he said, finding his own opening farther down the wall. 'Yeah, there's a couple men saddling up a bronc. Looks like they're going to take some kinks out some rough stock.'

Louie moved down so he could see both those leaning on a rail and the men working in the corral. In there, two men had the head of a smallish brown sorrel. They were holding it with a piece of blanket over the animal's eyes. A third man was trying to cinch a saddle on and was having a job of it. The horse might not have been able to see but it didn't like what was happening.

Finally saddled, the hand climbed on and got settled, holding the reins tight he nodded to the others. For a long moment after the blanket had been whipped away, the sorrel simply stood, head down. All of a sudden, like an explosion, it bucked. The rider was thrown, landing on his butt some distance away. The horse stopped and once again stood quietly with its head down, almost as if asleep. Buck could hear the men standing outside the corral laughing.

'What do ya think?' asked Louie.

'Not much we can do with all them there. Too many of them. Let's wait a bit and see what happens.'

Once again the horse's head was held while the hand swung into the saddle.

This time he didn't relax and when the horse bucked, he was ready. When the sorrel bucked, it'd put its head between its knees and pitch one way then the other. The rider pulled back on the reins and held the horse's head up. The bucking slowed as the horse tired. It wasn't long before the hand had the horse trotting around the corral.

Buck couldn't hear what the men standing around said, but three of them walked off, heading for the cabin. The fourth climbed into the corral to join the others.

'Keep an eye on them,' said Buck, then going to the front to watch the three men. He recognized two of them, Yarberry walking beside Fitzwalter. The third, he figured, had to be the outlaw the marshal was wanting, Neil something. He watched as they went into the cabin.

'I'm going to check those fellas out,' Louie said and went out the back door.

Not sure what his partner was up to, Buck went back across to watch. The men in the corral had stripped the sorrel and opened a gate to let it out. Turning, they looked back across the corral. They must have seen or heard Louie. Buck started to turn toward the back of the barn when he heard the cabin door open. Hesitating, he decided he'd better see what Yarberry was up to.

43

The gunfighter and the other man, the one Buck thought was probably the marshal's outlaw, came out the cabin door and walked across toward the big tree. Pulling a couple wood kitchen chairs around, they settled down and leaned back.

Seeing movement at the corner of the cabin, Buck saw Fitzwalter walk a short way disappearing into a small outhouse. Knowing where the three were, he headed toward the back of the barn. Just as he got to the door, Louie came in smiling.

'I had a little talk with the boys,' he said. 'I figured they were just hired hands and I was right. Don't think too much of their boss or his friends, either.'

'That was taking a chance.'

'Not really. I saw how those boys

were looking when Yarberry and the others laughed when that one fella got thrown.'

'So they agreed to stay out of it?'

Louie chuckled. 'They've decided there was some fences down in the south forty needing work. They're gone. One of them did mention something about if Fitzwalter were to get dead they would likely file on the place themselves.'

'Well, they'll have to wait. He isn't dead yet.'

'Uh huh. Yet,' said Louie, nodding toward the front of the barn. 'You come up with a plan?'

'There's two of them, the baddest ones I reckon, over under the tree. About the best I can think of is to simply walk out and brace them. Fitzwalter's busy in the outhouse and the other two are relaxing in the shade.'

Louie nodded. 'Might work. They won't be expecting us and maybe we'll get lucky.'

Checking the loads in first one

revolver then the other, Buck smiled. 'Isn't luck. We've got skill on our side.'

Slowly opening the double barn doors, the two men walked side by side toward the sitting men. Holding their revolvers at their side they got to about twenty feet from them before being spotted.

'Hey,' someone yelled. Yarberry came out of his chair, pulling his gun as he turned to face the intruders. Buck didn't hesitate. Taking the next step he raised his gun and shot the gunfighter. Yarberry got one shot off before crumbling, raising the dirt in front of Buck. Neil took two bullets from Louie's gun before falling.

The sudden silence fell like a blanket on the ranch yard. Buck and Louie stood looking down at the two bodies for a long heartbeat.

They whipped around when the cabin door slammed open and Fitzwalter come out running. The man was yelling, his face bunched in a grimace as he ran, firing his pistol at the men. Both Buck and Louie reacted, shooting the man in the chest.

Reloading, they holstered their weapons.

'I'll bring up the horses,' said Louie after a moment. Buck nodded. Going over he checked the two bodies under the tree. Both were dead. He didn't bother with Fitzwalter.

Riding down the ranch road toward the log gate, they saw horses off in the distance paying close attention to the two men. A meadowlark landed on a tall grass stem causing it to wave easily back and forth. Buck smiled at how peaceful everything seemed. Reaching the stage road they turned north.

'Won't make Fort Rawlins before late afternoon,' said Louie, rolling a smoke as they rode along. 'Sure makes my stomach growl, thinking it's been forgotten.'

'Uh huh,' Buck said after touching a match to his cigarette. 'It'll make supper that much better.' Slouching in the saddle they rode quietly, enjoying their smoke and the warm morning sun.

Buck broke the silence after a while. 'Guess we can tell the marshal where he can find his bad man.'

'Yeah, and we don't have to worry about Harry Yarberry or Issac Black coming up behind us neither. Except for the fact we ain't got a job to go to, life is pretty good.'

Buck nodded. He wasn't worried. As his grandma used to say, something would come up or it wouldn't.

We do hope that you have enjoyed reading this large print book.

Did you know that all of our titles are available for purchase?

We publish a wide range of high quality large print books including:
Romances, Mysteries, Classics
General Fiction
Non Fiction and Westerns

Special interest titles available in large print are:
The Little Oxford Dictionary
Music Book, Song Book
Hymn Book, Service Book

Also available from us courtesy of Oxford University Press:
Young Readers' Dictionary
(large print edition)
Young Readers' Thesaurus
(large print edition)

For further information or a free brochure, please contact us at:
Ulverscroft Large Print Books Ltd.,
The Green, Bradgate Road, Anstey,
Leicester, LE7 7FU, England.
Tel: (00 44) 0116 236 4325
Fax: (00 44) 0116 234 0205